# SEDUCTION BY TRUTH

# SEDUCTION BY TRUTH

Mukul Kumar

BLOOMSBURY
NEW DELHI • LONDON • OXFORD • NEW YORK • SYDNEY

BLOOMSBURY INDIA
Bloomsbury Publishing India Pvt. Ltd
Second Floor, LSC Building No. 4, DDA Complex, Pocket C – 6 & 7,
Vasant Kunj, New Delhi 110070

BLOOMSBURY, BLOOMSBURY PRIME and the Diana logo are
trademarks of Bloomsbury Publishing Plc

First published 2018



ISBN: 978-93-87457-62-1

2 4 6 8 10 9 7 5 3 1

Printed and bound in India by Replika Press Pvt Ltd

*Dedicated to*

*Lord Shiva*

# Contents

Acknowledgements ix

1. The Eclipse of Akriti 1
2. Shiva Sets Off on a Voyage 21
3. The Conquest of Sana 42
4. Resurrection of Deven 74
5. The Sliced Moon 89
6. Zeba Rises Like the Full Moon 107
7. The Fantasy Flight to Italy 133
8. Mary Flowers into a Lotus 161
9. Black Hole Turns Radiant 181

About the Author 189

# Acknowledgements

The Almighty—I am grateful to you for inspiring this work.

My Service—you are an eternal moral support.

VB Singh, my father—you sustained my belief in this work through your appreciation.

Shanti Singh, my mother—you have always believed in me.

Rakhi, my wife—you kept me motivated throughout this writing journey.

Avantika, my daughter—immense love for you, for being mine.

Payel Roy Chowdhury, my most demanding critic and a dear friend—your valuable suggestions have been immensely helpful in bringing roundness to the manuscript.

Manisha and Prabha—you were the great facilitators at home, making this gruel possible.

Khushi Ram, my typist—you brought my words to paper.

My friends and colleagues—thank you all for supporting, directly or indirectly, this precious venture.

Yogesh Sharma and Paul Vinay Kumar—you kept faith in me and my work.

Prita Maitra—your fine editing remarkably improved focus and crispness of the manuscript and made it reader-friendly. I shall always cherish the positive vibes from you.

Bloomsbury—you presented this book brilliantly.

And finally, and wholeheartedly, my readers—but for your love, support and appreciation through my writing journey thus far, this book wouldn't have been possible.

Thank you, all.

# The Eclipse of Akriti

*Extreme pain often leads you on a journey of discovery.*

The room glows through a sensuous translucent haze, providing a backlight to Shiva's figure as he moves around it, his heart throbbing, his blood racing. The atmosphere is a conscious effect created by Shiva, adjusting a vent here, a lamp there, to bathe his bedroom tonight in gold. Even the chill in the room has been conditioned to counter the Delhi summers, as well as the heat of his own body.

'Let's celebrate our grand coming to Delhi in a romantic way,' Shiva says to his wife, Akriti, his voice vibrant, his smile seductive, rarely so now, but familiar all the same. Now he is sitting up in bed with a look of anticipation. Akriti stands unmoving in front of the dressing table, moisturising her face, a twice-daily routine.

It is a fortnight since they have moved into their apartment and arranged it to their taste. Shiva and Akriti have paired up to add a uniquely tasteful décor to their new home, and such moments turn them conscious of the joy in their togetherness.

They are totally relaxed after having taken a post-dinner stroll in the finely manicured campus of their high-rise, and free from their son Ankur, who is sleeping comfortably in his room next door.

Happiness is known to stimulate one's body, mind, senses, all into animation, and Shiva is truly happy; he has grabbed an enviable position in the MNC of his choice, which has elevated him far above his peers. A graduate of IIM Ahmedabad, widely believed to be the top management school of India, Shiva worked hard to make his profile too formidable to be ignored. His exceptional inter-personal relations with the prominent people in the industry along with his inherent sophistication helped him no end to get him into the top management of the company. The new job had brought him back to Delhi, the city he loves. A Delhite—he did his schooling and college here—he has intensely fond memories of this city. Youth seems like a time of endless bliss to a man, and the place where it is spent is bound to remain dear to his heart. This job has also meant a plush flat with a big terrace garden in a posh high-rise complex in Gurgaon, the rapidly expanding business district in a suburb of Delhi. A coveted job in a coveted city—Shiva couldn't have asked for more.

'Frankly, I'm not in the mood, but if you are… Akriti says, instantly turning serious, letting her sentence trail off, being as gentle as possible lest Shiva feel hurt. She knows he is an extremely sensitive man.

'Oh, but I've never felt this alive in months,' says Shiva more quietly, the exuberance leaving his voice.

'Yes, but you weren't happy the last time. "No more easy and spontaneous lovemaking", you'd promised yourself. But if it's still fine with you, we can…' Again the sentence trailed. Akriti was now sitting on the bed, her tone defensive.

'I agree, there is no forgetting that, but…' Shiva is reflective, a tinge of sadness unmistakable in his eyes.

'—it's still a fact,' Akriti snatches away the words before Shiva can conclude. He is struck by the alacrity with which Akriti cuts short the rest of his sentence. It is explicit that she too has ceased to enjoy sex with him.

'Don't you think we should try to bring back those old feelings?' he asks, more quietly now. 'These days they have counselling for couples who feel the way we do.'

Akriti escapes into an uneasy pause, her eyes absentmindedly on the TV, which she has turned on to avoid looking at him and to demonstrate her lack of interest in relieving the rising tension.

Shiva senses her total disinterest, the hurt rising on his face. 'My friends are still making love to their wives,' he persists, 'of course not very frequently now. I understand desire gradually fades in marriage, but in our case we don't even try.' Somehow, the conviction is missing in his words. Shiva also turns to the screen, watching it blindly, in semi-defeat.

'You don't know the inside story; maybe they are imposing on their wives… who knows? Just the other day, my cousin Neelam painfully shared with me how Avinash forces himself upon her. But I know you are too sensitive to even think of that.' Akriti's unsettled tone is offensive and defensive at once.

'All said and done, our case has turned pathological,' Shiva begins to sound agitated. Akriti not appearing agreeable to his idea of finding ways to revive the passion in their marriage hurts his ego. For him now the issue is not sex, but Akriti lacking interest in *him*.

'And may I add something more without your getting hurt?' Akriti suddenly asks. She is fidgeting nervously in her place, placing a pillow needlessly on her lap for comfort that doesn't come.

'I knew it was Shiva-baiting time again!' his voice rising in irritation.

'You have been so touchy and impetuous, losing your temper at the slightest provocation, right since we got married. Faced with such tetchiness, how can a woman have any tender feelings left?' Agitation and a faint guilt mingle in Akriti's tone; guilt at depriving her spouse of sex, guilt that turns her defensive.

'For that matter, I too missed the wifely care and tenderness I expected from you. Yet, in those early days, the passion for each other never deserted us.'

'But then things were different, we were new to each other,' Akriti says, finally grasping the reality that novelty overpowered all rancour. Maybe she'd realised that all along but was only now vocalising it. Truth has a penchant for sitting deep inside, mostly settling at the bottom, and is disturbing to locate too, and that's why the inward journey to discover it is frightening.

'So now, finally, the truth comes out,' Shiva grins insincerely at Akriti as well as to himself. He loses further interest in the conversation, and switching off his bed lamp, slides down under the sheet, still restless.

'*I knew pretty well that, with time, one's passion gradually diminishes as the newness of the body opposite one wears off,*' he thinks to himself. '*But then why did I need Akriti to tell me this? Plus, somewhere down the line, even I was not sure that passion could be reignited with mere effort; I believed it had to be instantaneous. But still I pressed on all the same. Why? Did the husband in me dominate my rationality and question the wife who is supposed to offer herself up to her husband at his sweet will? Yes, tradition clashes with reason. And what about those occasions when I couldn't respond to Akriti's feelers, tired as I was after a long, punishing day at work?*'

Akriti, sensing Shiva's restiveness in the near-dark, whispers consolingly, 'Yes, novelty played its part for sure. But it's good that we are able to talk about this; most people don't and remain as if in a cauldron simmering with unease, or else drag the lovemaking into the long queue of the things which one does more as a matter of duty than choice, and come away from the experience dejected when the thrill eludes them yet again,' Akriti says, conviction now growing in her voice; the strength of truth elbowing away her guilt. She feels encouraged to be honest as Shiva never inflicted the torture of a dry conjugation upon her in spite of his occasional urges to connect.

Shiva remains silent, but a vague smile on his mellowed face scarcely visible in the near-dark room, brings some peace to Akriti. Bidding him a smiling 'goodnight', she quietly slips into sleep, while Shiva remains wistful, craving. '*Ah, how in those first impassioned days, we were hurled out of our silence into the blinding sport of passions*!' Earlier, such confusion between him and Akriti on the issue of sex simmered in him only for a short while. But an intense moment heats a simmer to a boil-over; here, sex not happening even amidst all the other reasons to rejoice—a prized career move, a beautiful house and cushy perks, and that too after a long gap! Tonight he begins to believe that sex has, alas, made a permanent exit from his marriage and any return is ruled out. Shiva switches off the remaining lights and tries to sleep. But sleep eludes him for a long time before settling on his eyelids—and even then, only lightly.

A disturbed sleep leaves imprints of weariness on Shiva's face next morning but he tries to look normal. Akriti, sensing his discomfort, tries to be a bit more pleasant to him, which her husband quickly senses. She sends Ankur to school before joining her husband for breakfast, which has not been a must for her in the past. Tension still hangs in the air. Finally, Shiva leaves for office. He picks up the newspaper to read in the car; he normally carries at least one to relieve the boredom of long traffic jams, and to alleviate his worries. 'Depriving Husband of Sex May Be Legal Ground for Divorce' leaps up in bold headlines from the newspaper he is reading. Last night's thoughts assail him again: '*How can a wife be forced against her will to have sex with her husband? It's tyrannical. If a husband forces himself upon his wife, it is marital rape. But then what course to tread? Can dharma dictate his having to bear the constant deprivation of the fulfilment of man's most basic drive? No, rationally speaking, it can't do that. In Hindu tradition, kama was right up there along with dharma, as belonging to the four goals in human life. Traditionally, the theory of sex in marriage only for procreation defies my reason, as it challenges the chemistry of the human body which may demand sex even after. So, when marriage can't sustain passion, is the fulfilment of desire outside marriage the only recourse? But tradition says that is taboo...*' Torn apart by these riotous thoughts, Shiva is in a vortex of indecision. And how could he not be emotionally disturbed as well under the circumstances?

Shiva is a man with a keen intellect, is sensitive and thoughtful. Knowledge of different people and their traditions naturally fascinate him. Immensely fond of reading books on history and mythology, he often searches for answers to such baffling questions that life throws up.

He reaches office and flings himself down into his chair in his chamber.

'Good morning, Sir. You have a meeting at noon and I am done with the paperwork,' says Sana. Sana is the personal secretary of Shiva. She is pretty adept at handling routine affairs even when her boss needs to travel on official work, within the country as well as overseas.

'Sorry, Sana, I am a bit unwell. I will tell Prashant to attend the meeting. He's the one, anyway, who has to make the presentation on the new project before the investors. I have already seen it. I will join them right at the end for the summing-up discussion.' Shiva's voice is shorn of its typical baritone.

'Right, Sir, I will brief Mr Prashant accordingly.' She adds, 'Shall I get a cup of coffee for you? You look tired.' Sana is standing right across the desk, and has noticed how weary he looks.

'So nice of you, thanks,' Shiva keeps it brief. He reclines in his chair, his mind refusing to go into work mode.

'Right away, Sir,' she says. Shiva watches Sana as she leaves the room, thinking, fondly, '*How caring she is, and meticulous in her work as well*!' He's always thought well of her, but today his appreciation of her qualities is marked.

Sana is a smartly turned-out woman, fortyish, fairly tall, and always dresses to the suit the corporate standards perfectly. She looks like a woman who works hard to keep in shape, and has trained herself to adopt the perfect secretary walk—conveying both efficiency and a subtle feminity. But Shiva has often felt that the demands of the job have, over time, chiseled her body language into a robotic gait, stopping her womanliness from blossoming fully.

'Your coffee, Sir.' She has returned quickly, the office boy in tow, and gestures to him to place Shiva's customary mug on the desk.

'Thanks.'

'Try to relax, Sir. I'll call you only if something urgent turns up.'

Shiva sips his coffee, his mind now completely fixated upon the thought of sex lacking in his life for quite a while now, and sparkling sex still longer. He leans back in his chair again, shuts his eyes and finds himself caught up in nostalgic memories of satisfying sex with Akriti. The slog to reach this position in his career had somehow kept this consciousness at bay so far, but today there is nothing to check it. Sipping his coffee, he remains under the spell of those memories.

The coffee finally does him some good, jerking him

back to his work. He rises from his chair, unusually cold from the direct blast of the air conditioner, and shifts his seat to catch some of the brilliant sunshine coming in through the unprotected window to his left. The sudden view of the bustling roads down below helps to revive his spirits. He opens his laptop and begins to work.

It's a while before a gentle knock at the door breaks his concentration. 'Sir, the presentation is over. You are awaited in the conference room. Hope you're feeling better?' asks Sana solicitously.

'Yeah, let's go.' But Shiva rises slowly from his chair, trying to shed the lingering reluctance to spring into action. He pulls himself together and briskly enters the conference room, greets everyone briefly and sums up the presentation in his usual convincing style. It is a style which has earned him considerable admiration over the years—and some envy, too. Work, Shiva is eternally passionate about. And it has never let him down.

Shiva returns home, feeling more like himself. The reasoned self-examination over the day has flushed out the resentment against his wife. Akriti asks the maid to fetch the tea and sandwiches that have been prepared, and inquires after her husband's day. He responds with apparent normalcy. He goes in to change his clothes before joining her in the living room. The two have their tea together, and then Shiva takes the lift down to the underground rink to watch Ankur skating with his friends. He even tries to skate a few circles of the rink at the insistence of his son. The children all laugh and applaud; the father-son bond sparkles. The rest of the evening progresses as usual, with Ankur's homework, their dinner, postprandial stroll, Shiva working on his laptop and finally, his customary read in the living room. Tonight he reads longer than usual, into the late hours, before retiring to bed, quietly joining Akriti who is already asleep. Ankur sleeps in his own room.

The life of the family resumes its normal rhythm.

However, despite his ordinary behaviour, Shiva remains constantly haunted by the feeling that his life is deficient, especially when his sexual urge spikes. Restlessness had already become the norm in his existence. But now that sex with his wife appears precluded altogether from the scene, his unease is underscored. His mind remains caught up in the conflict between rationality and tradition, between sex and marriage, without throwing up a conclusive win of one over the other.

It is almost six months since they came to Delhi.

Throughout them all, Sana's caring presence has never failed to soothe his restive mind, and at times, even raised some exciting flutters in him.

But they are only momentary. Sooner or later, he returns to his previous state of frustration. Of late, he has noticed that Akriti is increasingly occupied with her mobile phone, also tending to guard it like a hawk, avoiding sparing it even for Ankur's occasional games. A vague suspicion prickles in his mind, but he tries to drive it out, rationalising it with all those 'maybes'—'maybe she and her friends need to share some intimate girlie jokes between them; maybe, maybe, maybe...'

But this suspicion turns thornier one evening when he notices Akriti engrossed in her mobile for minutes on end, with an obvious blush suffusing her face, refusing to get off even when he has only just returned from office. His suspicion quickly grows full-blown: '*Is she having an affair*?'

He keeps mum, deciding to observe her longer. Somehow, Shiva finds the thought of checking her mobile too distasteful. But the suspicion sets in more firmly.

'*But*,' he scolds himself silently, '*what if she is not*? *It's neither fair nor dignified to accuse her on the basis of mere suspicion*.' The thought keeps him from asking her upfront. Instead, he decides to take an oblique way. He has been struck by an article in a new issue of his favourite magazine. The title, which drew him to it, was 'Sex in Marriage & Adultery'.

'Did you read that article on adultery?' Shiva casually asks Akriti, showing her the magazine over tea one evening.

'Yes, I read it, only in bits, though,' she says, just as lightly. They both know Akriti doesn't have the patience to read anything through.

'It says that, these days, both spouses feel pressed to seek sexual fulfilment outside marriage... boredom with the partner, you know.'

'It's not a big deal,' Akriti says casually, her voice cool.

'What if I agreed that seeking sex outside marriage was OK? Our marriage, anyway... you know what I mean,' Shiva says with a faint smile, strategically blending his gravity with a look of mischief.

'What should I say? If you're fine with it, then...' Akriti shrugs the non-comittally.

Finding her both normal and at the same time sensing a kind of permissiveness lurking behind her words, Shiva's smoothening feathers are ruffled again. He pretends to be more absorbed in the magazine to convey his disinterest in the matter.

But his mind shouts: '*Is Akriti's lack of interest in me so complete that it has pushed her to extent of permitting me an affair? Or is she seeing someone and is trying to legitimatise hers? Also, Akriti is not exactly an orthodox woman. She's told me so often, "I wouldn't want anyone to be stifled by societal norms". As a man, my mind can appreciate her rationality, but as a husband this lack of possessiveness hurts! Maybe, the verdicts of conscience and tradition are bound to be different.*' The silence grows cacophonous, and Shiva feels too uneasy to remain in the apartment.

'I'll go downstairs and catch up with Ankur,' Shiva says, finishing his tea.

But Shiva doesn't go to Ankur. Instead, he sets himself adrift, walking aimlessly in the premises, his hands inside the pockets of his suede jacket for warmth. It is winter now, and the chill is creeping in.

Suspicion torments him. And then, suddenly, a thrill rises to mingle with his torment; his mind turns conscious of his wife's covert permissiveness, also implying his own extramarital affair turning legitimate. He feels a growing excitement. Sex outside marriage had already been a sneaking option in his mind—now it returns with increasing vigour. Shiva remains in the grip of this bizarre pull between torment and thrill for a longish while. He becomes aware of the darkening dusk and decides to go back to his flat. Kaleidoscope is the new colour of his thoughts.

Shiva and Akriti are taking their post-dinner stroll in the campus while Ankur is skating under the floodlights in the pleasantness of the March spring; he has just finished his exams.

'Mummy, mummy...' they hear Ankur scream.

Shiva and Akriti race to the rink. Ankur is on the

ground, holding his bent leg and crying. They hurry up to him to find his knee bleeding profusely, the sight of blood amplifying the dread in their mind. They try to make him get up, but he resists out of apparently acute pain.

'Oh! It's really a bad one. I told you not to skate without your guards on, now...' Akriti gets mother-panicky. She peers at the wound, praying it is not a deep one. Please not, a fracture.

'Wait, let me go upstairs and bring some cotton wool and antiseptic,' Shiva says, already rushing off.

He goes upstairs, unlocks the door and enters his flat, still in a frenzy. He manages to find the first-aid box, grabs it, but just when he is ready to hurry back, he hears the beep of a message on the mobile charging at Akriti's bedside table. Shiva stops to have a quick look. 'Tomorrow,' it reads, 'at 11, same place, love you XXX.' Shiva stands frozen. He can't read the full message as the mobile is locked; he is not sure whether he would have, even if he could. For a fleeting while 'the bleeding son' in his mind gets overwritten by 'an adulterous wife', 'a promiscuous woman'—that is what she appears at this moment. The rage drives him dizzy. He shuts his eyes hard, clenches his jaws and tightens his body to regain control over himself, wishing to forget all in a flash. The 'bleeding son' flashes back and jolts the immobilised husband out into reality, and he rushes back to his wounded child.

'God forbid, but what if the poor boy has broken his knee?' one of the residents standing around Ankur is saying anxiously.

'Why is he not able to stand up?' Akriti is tearfully jittery. Shiva, in a strong, fatherly act, cleans the wound; Ankur is constantly flinching away from the sting of the astringent.

'It'll be all right, he is a brave boy,' Shiva feigns normalcy, and is almost comically masterful.

The first-aid complete, Shiva tries to support Ankur so he can walk on his own to their apartment, but Ankur is just not able to stand up. Eventually, Shiva lifts his son in his arms and heads home, apprehending a cracked patella. Once back in their bedroom, Akriti remains glued to Ankur's side, caressing her baby to sleep, unmoving despite two more bleeps on her mobile. This soothes Shiva a bit, like the warm fomentation on an angry boil. He realises that though 'social stigma' and 'structural chaos' matter, a 'child' alone may be sufficient reason for continuing in a marriage; if not as wife and husband, at least as the child's mother and father.

Once Ankur has stopped crying, they make a quick trip, Shiva tenderly carrying Ankur to the orthopaedic doctor at the hospital where they are registered. An X-ray is taken, confirming that Ankur's pain arises from a slight hairline fracture, requiring nothing but plaster and a few days of inaction to heal. 'Just a greenstick!' the surgeon reassures them jovially. Relieved, but still not engaging his wife in conversation, Shiva drives them home and he retires to bed—but tonight in Ankur's room. Akriti is with her son in the master bedroom, invoking the therapeutic power of her maternal instincts. Shiva is amazed at his own silent reaction to the discovery of his wife's adultery. He remains wide-awake, frightened to shut his eyes, lest terrible memories of the evening return with the darkness behind his lids. He rises from bed, heads to the drawing room and switches the lights on. Suddenly, his eyes fall upon his reflection in the antique mirror on the wall fiercely staring at him. He stands stock-still in front of it, noticing his thinning hair, the discernible paunch, the plumpish face swallowing the jaw line and replacing it with a double chin. His image shoots uncomfortable questions at him: '*Do you look as handsome as before? Has your neglected body also contributed to Akriti's lack of attraction to you*?' He is filled with horrifying thoughts, breeding heart-wrenching feelings. And then comes the worst one of them all: '*Is the one she is seeing more handsome than me*?'

Shiva veers away from the mirror towards the bar, pours himself a single malt and walks out on to the terrace. He looks at the sky to amplify his solitude, but finding the smog shrouding the starry apron, his gaze drops down to the ground which is bathed in neon. The distant whirr of vehicles heightens the silence and stillness of the night. His mind returns to the old worrisome topic: '*How handsome I was in my heyday! How I enjoyed commanding the attention of all those girls!? And now...?*'

Shiva is six feet tall, with a broad frame tapering to a perfect V at his hips, leading to long, sturdy legs. Somewhere along the way, an expanding waistline has distorted the angles and added the unmasculine roundedness. He is fair-complexioned with Aryan features, sharp and defined, big eyes and a remarkably bow-shaped mouth. The inherent boyishness of his face has survived the ravages of time, making him look younger than he is. In his youth, he had taken care to dress to accentuate his physique and flamboyant carriage. Besides, he had been a masterful debater, having won many competitions in college. And a keen interest in mythology and history had made his repertoire of logic more fascinating. The blend of his looks and intellect had combined to make him a charismatic persona. Even now he stands out in a crowd.

His reflections continue to pass through his mind in a procession, queuing up for attention, '*Was Akriti right when she said my anger played a role in diminishing our sex life? She went to the extent of calling my presence in the house demonic when I shouted at Ankur for faltering in his studies, or when I am disgruntled with the slightest hint of disturbance in the rhythm of life at home. I have to admit she remains cool and composed no matter what life serves up to her; how aptly she always says that regret will not change the flavour of the platter. But then did I also not miss the sensitivity she once possessed? Even when she shows care for me I believe she's acting out of duty rather than concern for my feelings—her ways can set the mind in order, but leave the heart craving.'*

Ultimately, his mind tries to make him see sense. '*Am I merely confused? Were we not the same earlier? She has already confessed that we were new to each other then. Akriti, like me, might have grown bored with the sameness of body, and behaviour as well, and maybe that is why… but was she so desperate for a change so as to violate the sacramental bond? Look at the way she hides her mobile like a stolen treasure. Count how many frequent and unexplained trips she makes out of the house! I used to think women were the shyer sex.'*

Far from being reassured, as Shiva had set out to be, he feels shredded by his conflicting thoughts. Ultimately, he surrenders all hope. He repairs to the bar, pours himself a second drink and comes back to the terrace. He is sipping his scotch, his pensive glances wandering in the void. The scotch by now is rising to his head, deepening the melancholy and amplifying the infinity in his mind. Sadness, juxtaposed with alcohol, usually does that to a man: it turns his thoughts to doubtful contemplations about marriage, relationships, pain, pleasure, the intricacies of life… Shiva gulps down his drink in one long, desperate swallow, trying to completely drown out his thoughts, then returns to Ankur's bedroom, and lies down on the bed.

His slumber is plagued by hallucinations, images of Akriti's body in someone else's bed, mercilessly stabbing it. And always, always, the dark silhouette of a man, unknown to him, keeps lurking ominously in the shadows behind it.

He looks awful in the morning. Akriti relates the dark circles under his eyes to anxiety over Ankur's injury the night before. Shiva and Akriti spend the next day getting their son medically re-examined and treated. Through it all, Shiva does not let Akriti sense his knowledge of her affair. Apprehension is vocal while acceptance is silent.

But silence does not necessarily mean inaction.

☒

# Shiva Sets Off on a Voyage

Their ordinary routine is resumed the next day. Shiva is getting ready for office, wrapped in sullenness. This morning, Akriti can easily sense that it is not Ankur's hairline fracture alone which is bothering him; coexistence tends to breed the sixth sense.

'You look pale,' observes Akriti. 'You musn't worry. Ankur will be fine soon.' Akriti is trying to be pleasant to him; the intent really being to find out what is truly troubling him.

'I'm fine,' Shiva mumbles, entering the washroom.

'*He is withdrawn and subdued, something is terribly wrong. Has he sniffed out my secret*?' Akriti is suddenly struck by the ugly likelihood. '*No, it can't be, he's too impulsive to let it go so quietly*,' she tries to console herself. She knows only too well how Shiva is the one given to instant eruptions of fury.

After his bath, he remains preening for a while in the mirror, consciously trying to do himself up better than usual. He brushes his hair generously to lend an air of thickness to it, trying to comb the longer strands to their optimum reach over his head to cover the thin patch in the middle of his crown. All the while, the image of the younger Shiva's rich and bouncy waves mocks him in the looking glass. After putting on an oxford blue linen suit with a swagger, the older Shiva takes another, longer, look at himself, trying to draw his paunch in by holding in his breath. '*It's still not alarming, just a few days of exercise will send it back*,' he tells his reflection encouragingly. At breakfast, he turns aware of Akriti's own appearance, and thinks, '*She still looks charming despite putting on a couple of kilos over the years—in fact that has added to her general oomph. But why am I suddenly obsessed with comparing our looks*?'

Akriti is a beautiful woman. Her golden skin and brown hair lend a Western shade to an otherwise north Indian look, and the pride she takes in her home, and the care she lavishes on her friends, her family, lend a reassuring Indian aura to her attraction.

Before leaving for office Shiva goes in to see Ankur; they spend together a few affectionate moments before Shiva leaves, patting his back and saying, 'My brave boy, you'll be fine soon.' Ankur smiles and waves him goodbye.

Shiva crawls past the gleaming glass-fronted high-rises of Gurgaon. His car is caught in an inevitable traffic jam—stopping, driving for a few precious metres, stopping again. Akriti never leaves his mind. He begins to wonder if his wife ever loved him, or if love in a marriage was asking for too much. Disturbed anew, he turns his eyes to the newspaper beside him. The report of a 'Protest Over Rising Intolerance in the Country' transports him back to his IIM Ahmedabad days. He had joined it a little after the infamous Gujarat riots in 2002.

Kishor, Ritesh and he are standing at the roadside stall, Al Arabi, famous for its authentic Lebanese shawarma. While the helpers prepare the rolls, the owner of the stall gets into an animated chat with the three students. They tell him they have come for the first time to his stall, to test his fame. The owner is a street-smart man, brimming with pride in his art and eternally eager to talk about it.

'This fellow placed his order at 4 in the evening for five rolls. He was supposed to collect them at 7. It is already 7:45, and now I will not meet his order. Instead, I have decided to give it to you. Otherwise, I wouldn't be able to make your order, since you haven't ordered it in advance.' The shawarma man makes the threesome realise how lucky they have got this evening.

'How old is your stall?' asks Shiva, amused by his style.

'Just two years. Before this I lived in Saudi Arabia for twelve years. I was working in a big restaurant, and when I wanted to leave, they were not prepared to let me go. But I am too good to remain behind the scenes, I wanted to run my own show at my own place. By the way, I am known as Tariq Khan,' he says, flicking his collar upwards.

'OK, Tariq, delighted to meet you,' says Kishor.

The rolls are served.

'Hmmm, amazing, simply delicious,' Shiva sounds genuinely impressed; the others nod in agreement, their mouths full.

Seeing Tariq turn to Ritesh and Kishor to deliver a fresh burst of self-praise, Shiva reflects, 'People like Tariq Khan are designed in the mould of happiness; how easy being happy can be!'

While Tariq is busy chatting to his audience of three, his helpers serve the other customers.

Tariq carries on, uninterruptedly loud and animated. 'Let me tell you, sirs, the secret of my fabulous shawarma is the mayonnaise which I prepare with my own hands. It's hell to manually prepare such a huge quantity, you can see how fast I need to prepare and sell in these vast numbers.'

The three exchange smiles which say, '*Tariq is so glib—but interesting*!'

'He just gave us MBA guys two real lessons in business management,' Kishor observes to Shiva. 'One, it is always handmade things that are most valued because they are products of passion, not mere process. And two, advertisement has to be loud enough to get the most out of it. Look at the attention he's grabbing from everyone around!'

Shiva tries to get Tariq to give credit where it's due.

'But your boys truly make things easy for you,' he tells the shawarma vendor. 'They do things to your standards; and how young they are to learn so much!'

'Sir, let me tell you something very interesting. They are the sons of one of my very good friends. He is a staunch brahmin, his family doesn't even touch meat, nor do these boys. My friend fell into some really bad times. When I came back from Saudi Arabia and set up this stall, it picked up sales in no time, and I needed some help. Then he offered the services of his two sons, knowing that with me they will be able to earn some money. And since I set up my stall only in the evening, they are able to continue to attend school in the morning, and as for their being young, I believe that hunger is the best recipe for cooking well.' The swagger in Tariq's voice mellows into somberness.

'Muslims and brahmins coming together, and that too in this state, which recently saw one of the bloodiest ever riots!' Shiva exclaims.

'Sir, you learn ideals in your books, we live them on the ground,' Tariq says.

'The ideals came from the books to the ground, or vice versa?' wonders Shiva.

'And God comes only after hunger,' intones Tariq, meaningfully.

Shiva, returns his attention to the shawarma. 'Why

don't you start a business in Delhi?' he asks Tariq, still chewing. 'Delhi-ites are big foodies, you'll earn huge amounts of money.' Shiva takes his last bite.

'No way, sir, I am happy at my place with the money I earn and…' suddenly, Tariq hushes his tone, moves swiftly towards the threesome to ensure he is audible only to them and continues, 'and sir, I have a girlfriend here, we only met a year ago.' Tariq beams an impish smile.

'You are unmarried?' Ritesh looks surprised.

'Sir, I am very much married with two kids. But I still have a girlfriend. We can meet only after midnight, as that is how late I work so that I can earn adequate money for my wife—that is all she needs now from me. You know, we have been married for thirteen years. Thus, up to midnight I live for my family, and after that I live for my desire.'

'But does your wife not…' Shiva says, looking curious. The three are truly amused. Kishor says, 'And how does the girl manage to meet you so late at night…'

Tariq takes over, getting at what the boys wished to know, 'One has to manage. Even a short meeting with her freshens me up and my girlfriend lives alone.' Tariq pauses for a while before saying emphatically, 'Sirs, my funda is clear: life means a balance between marriage, desire and money, a bit less of everything makes life complete,' Tariq looks a postcard picture of a contented man who is free from any doubts.

At this juncture in this fleeting reel of his student days, Shiva finds himself fast-forward into the present, reflecting, '*Ah, now I realise the meaning of what Tariq said then! Does Akriti too wants only money and security from marriage? But I believed both of us feel attachment for each other in spite of our incompatibilities; a decade of togetherness is bound to induce it. But how could Tariq be so sure of his wife seeking only money from him? He could strike such a fine balance between marriage and desire, but did his wife too fall for someone else...?*' Caught up in his wild imaginings, he sees he has reached his office.

Shiva runs a sweeping gaze over his colleagues, keenly examining a few of those who zealously greet him, and feeling comforted by the thought that he still looks better than many.

'Sir, you have an important meeting this afternoon regarding the overseas project,' Sana has arranged his desk for the day. Shiva, by virtue of his experience in marketing and project management, has been assigned the responsibility for the crucial overseas ventures of the company.

'Thanks,' Shiva's acknowledgment is deliberately short, hinting at wanting to be left alone. Trouble may be helped by sharing, but tragedy can be tackled only in solitude.

'Shall send some green tea in a short while,' Sana says brightly, and makes a quiet exit; she has perfected the art of attending to her boss, understanding what is said and what is left unsaid at once. She has also found Shiva, even in the short time she's known him, highly appreciative of the personal touch she adds to her behaviour. He wonders sometimes if she had done the same with her previous bosses as well.

With Sana gone, Shiva reclines in his chair, looking up at the false ceiling, then swivels round his chair to the big glass window at his back to look into the sky and ponder over the hellish events of that fateful evening. '*Should I check Akriti, wielding the stick as a husband should, when I have decided to continue with her in spite of her infidelity? Many Hindu scriptures profess that men should control women lest they overstep the marital boundary, which I call traditional masculinity. But that way I may stop only her body but not her heart from leaping out to land into someone else's lap. And what if only her body has eloped and her heart has stayed back? Her body, anyway, I had lost, we had stopped making love. And I feel stopping her would destroy my self-respect. A man should win the woman, even if she is his wife, rather than control her…*' The thoughts keep churning in him for a long while until the course of action for him is precipitated.

'*But still I feel miserable,*' his self protests, '*not in losing her body, but losing her body to another man! The "husband" in me gets venomously angry at the thought of a reasoned reconciliation with my wife's adultery. A man wants to possess the body of his wife, than her heart. However, instead of tradition I feel like living with my intellect which tells me that sex and marriage invariably clash with each other after the initial novelty between the spouses wears off, and their incompatibilities begin to cause the first friction. Other couples must have discovered the same. So let me try to test this out empirically on other couples.*

*And, like Akriti, I too shall fulfil my passions now, and prove to myself that I am still desirable; it will channel my anger and satisfy my burning need for revenge, indirect though it may be. These two goals, satisfying my passions, and discovering other marriages, can be attained at once if I win over only married women to help me with my research. Won't that be intellectual masculinity?*

*I still look better than most; I will regain my youthful looks with a new hairstyle, exercises and grooming, and I can. I am only forty-one, and my sophistication never fails to charm people. But I will invent the logic to establish only the truths I believe. And yes, this journey of discovery will be fun at the very least…'* The prospect of treading the path of guilt-free extramarital relationships instantly sends a tide of excitement through Shiva momentarily, dispelling his angst. '*Do I want to break those women's marriages because someone broke mine? Won't it be sinister to entrap other women to settle a personal score with Akriti?*' But he quickly pulls himself out of such polemics and sets about drawing up a plan.

The clink of the saucer on the table brings him back to consciousness; he didn't even hear the earlier gentle knock on the door by the office boy. He wasn't even aware when, while gazing at the sky, he had shut his eyes and reclined into his chair. As Shiva wheels his chair back and tries to lift the cup, he experiences a sudden giddiness and a blurring of vision. The stormy findings of self-awareness have not yet settled in. He lifts the cup and deeply gazes at the tea in it; he misses the old appeal of the shimmery hue of the cocktail of green tea and the sun filtering through his window; it's not eyes but the mind which senses the beauty. Just when he forces himself to take a sip, his phone rings.

'Sir,' says Sana hesitantly, 'sorry to disturb you, but Mr Prashant wants to speak to you urgently.'

'Please put him on the line.'

'Right, Sir, it was important, otherwise…' Sana sounds almost guilty.

'No issue, please…'

Following the conversation, Shiva's thoughts again turn to Sana. '*Sana was reluctant to put me on line to Prashant. She was only doing her duty. How sensitive she is*!'

Sana comes in just a while later to seek Shiva's views on fixing the official appointment with a company regarding a project. Shiva looks at her pretty face, feeling the faint beginnings of a strange attraction for her; her peaches-and-cream complexion, her large expressive eyes emphasised by kajal, the red of her carefully lipsticked mouth, her perfect grooming and manners, her sleekly-bound long thick hair with a few loose tendrils caressing her forehead and cheeks heightening her Punjabi voluptuousness. '*But doesn't her heavy make-up lend a touch of artificiality to her appearance*?' crosses his mind.

In the afternoon, Shiva has to meet his counterpart, the project head of another company with which his company has formed a joint venture for the new overseas project; it is to set up an integrated crude oil exploration and processing plant in Baku, the capital city of Azerbaijan. Oil has been as eternally crucial to India as it has been to all countries, and it remains an attractive area of investment. Baku is emerging as an oil hub as the Government of Azerbaijan intends to exploit the oil reserves lying untapped there thus far to propel itself on to a high-growth trajectory. The company is in the process of preparing a Detailed Project Report (DPR).

'Sir, Mr Prashant is joining us in a short while for the meeting. Do you need any assistance?' Sana is sitting on a chair across his desk.

'Sana, you are accompanying me to the meeting. I want you to record the discussions to ensure that our viewpoint gets adequately reflected in the minutes. Hope that's fine with you?' Shiva steals a glance at the slim line of vermilion adorning the parting of her hair, with a discreet smile.

'As you wish, Sir, but I have hardly been taken to such meetings before.' Sana is visibly happy; it is a break in the monotony of the usual office day for her.

'A beginning has to be made sometime; let it be today.' Shiva gives her a superior smile.

'I think the meeting with Ms Zeba's team was pretty productive, and courtesy you, we could finalise the outcome then and there. I hope now we can straightaway finalise the DPR. And yes, you were amazing today! I can't believe it was your debut participation; you could artfully cull out my intent from the discussions without much of my intervention,' Shiva says to Sana animatedly; the meeting is over, and they are in the lift. Prashant has stayed back for some more work.

'Sir, thanks for your kind words of appreciation.' Sana feels surprised at Shiva's demeanour, thinking, '*Usually he is so measured in his expressions, never talks lightly, is slow to smile, but today there is this sudden surge of pleasantries.*'

'Sana, you deserve that. I am surprised at your familiarity with even the technical aspects of our work.' Shiva seems deeply concentrated on her.

They proceed to Shiva's car and leave for their office. Shiva realises Sana is uneasy with his new sociable avatar, but he knows what he's doing.

He resolves to complete the journey he has undertaken—from a 'blazing Akriti' to a 'glowing Sana'; the fire untamed is macabre, the fire tamed is life.

'Sir, it was you who guided the discussion to definite conclusions; you deliberately avoided the peripherals, I keenly watched everything. I hardly deserve any credit for it,' Sana says buoyantly; blushing with the attention given to her by her boss, and elated at being a part of something important for her company. However, she pushes the sudden thaw in the boss's cool demeanour to the back of her mind.

'Oh heck, it's quite late, I'll wrap up,' Shiva says entering the office. 'How do you commute? In your own car?'

'I don't drive, I commute in either my colleague's car or my husband's, when he is in town, and free; otherwise I take a cab. I live nearby and that makes things a bit easier for me,' Sana says while accompanying him into his chamber, the pace in her walk and words conveying aloud her hurry to get home; women are inherently timed to the routine of living.

'It's a bit late. If it's fine with you, I'll drop you home if your colleague has already left.' He is winding up while talking, Sana glowing brighter in his mind.

'Thanks, Sir, I'll take a cab. You needn't take the trouble.'

'I am the reason for your delay, you are coming with me.'

She yields.

'Tell me about your family,' Shiva takes his place in the back seat of his car, with Sana beside him. The driver has been given Sana's address.

'My husband is in trade; he deals in computer parts, connects the suppliers to the retailers. I have a daughter, she is studying in the Indian Institute of Management, Bangalore,' Sana says, still feeling uneasy.

'Great, that means she's doing well! Does her joining an IIM have anything to do with your working in an MNC?' Shiva asks smilingly.

'Not exactly, but being closer to her mother, she has listened to me talking very highly about my bosses, how they enjoy a wide exposure and dazzling pay packets. That may have inspired her, but I never forced it upon her, nor did her father.'

'Hmm, so you must be missing her, more so as she is a mama's girl.'

'Yes, and my husband also is mostly out on business tours. I tend to feel pretty lonely at times.'

'Lonely'—Sana's use of the word opens up exciting possibilities in Shiva's newly adventurous mind.

'Honestly, you look too young to have a daughter studying in an IIM,' Shiva's eyes twinkle with a faint coquetry; he knows women love to think they look younger than they are and such compliments instantly tickle them to heaven. He knows what he said is not untrue, but yes, he has said this to serve a definite end.

Sana's brightens up, her amazement at this new side to her boss growing further.

'Actually, I was married very young and had my daughter just a little more than a year after.'

'Oh, somehow the thought of women having babies so young makes me uncomfortable…' Shiva suddenly checks himself from speaking further on this; the rest of his thoughts remain in his mind. 'Making a wife a mother so early is one of the many ways men subjugate women,' he finally says.

Shiva notices Sana growing a bit sombre, the delighted smile on her face now tremulous.

'I mean, it's very difficult to manage the responsibilities of child-rearing when one is a novice. That is the time to taste the freedom of youth.' Shiva notices her face grow graver.

She falls silent, looking out through the window away from Shiva. Shiva feels a prick of guilt.

'Please stop ahead on the left, a little short of the

square,' Sana says to the driver, breaking the uncomfortable silence.

'Why here? We will drop you inside the premises,' Shiva sounds apprehensive in case he has caused Sana anxiety in any way.

'It's all right, I will get down here,' Sana insists.

She takes leave of him with a humble 'Thank you'. Shiva watches her fondly as she walks away. He relishes her lingering fragrance in the car. As he draws closer home, Akriti springs to his mind with an awkward suddenness, causing him both pain and an unfamiliar fear—the fear of the sight of her reignites his intense anger. He tries to recover his composure, remembering Ankur, societal norms, material order in life, and the positives of Akriti's cheerful disposition, and his fear is replaced by sorrow.

By the time Shiva reaches home he tries his best to behave normally, which puts Akriti at ease. But looking at her directly enrages him all over again—till he recollects his own plan to indulge all the passion he has suppressed so far with gleeful abandon.

Tea, a little fussing over Ankur's fractured leg, dinner, scheduled official work at home, sleep—repeatedly broken by haunting thoughts of Akriti's adultery, making it a night of multiple waking dawns. The actual morning catapults him into his gym. He sweats it out with a vengeful fury, recalling the looks which won him the attention of girls in his youth.

'It is good you resumed exercising. You were putting on a bit of weight,' Akriti says to Shiva after he gets back from the gym, surveying him critically.

'Hmmm, I will have to hurry to the office,' Shiva says smiling a brief smile.

'Breakfast is ready, have a quick bath,' Akriti tries to sound more involved in his welfare than usual.

'I will.' Shiva enters the washroom. Inside, his distress shows up on the steam on the glass walls and surfaces. He grooms himself even more carefully than the last time in front of the mirror, and nods approvingly to himself. He has already decided to go in for a new hairstyle.

'Sir, I have finished the Record of Discussion of yesterday's meeting. You can have a look before I mail it to Mr Prashant to take it forward,' Sana says, smiling wider at Shiva this morning.

'Okay, Sana, I will do that. Meanwhile, would you please proof a draft of mine? I'll mail it to you right away.' Shiva's glibness is unmistakably suggestive of his advances to her—and he knows it.

'Sure, Sir, anything else?' Sana reciprocates his zeal.

'So nice of you—nothing else for now.' When she is at the door, Shiva says, almost simpering, with his head coquettishly tilted, 'By the way, that parrot-green sari suits you a lot.' Shiva thinks sari multiplies the oomph factor in women. She has decked herself up, emboldened by the thrill of the attention 'Sir' has been showering on her lately.

Sana blushes a deep red, uttering a gleeful 'Thanks!' Shiva feels happy watching his overtures taking effect. While she exits this time, his gaze is more intensely directed at her alluringly fulsome hips, their sinuous sway, reminding him of Reubens' *Venus in Front of the Mirror* and the subject's voluptuous buttocks—Shiva often wonders whether he suffers from fat fetishism. With his interest in mythology and history, he has come to extend his fascination to art and paintings, particularly those of the Renaissance era, depicting women in all their unapologetic and billowing nudity. He enjoys viewing these creations on YouTube, craving to see the originals up close someday; he passionately nurses the wish to visit Italy, the hub of Renaissance art, which his official overseas itineraries haven't covered so far. The Vatican Museum, particularly the Sistine Chapel and the incomparable works of Michelangelo—he yearns to see them all. And now this wish may soon become a reality because the new project he is working on involves a visit to Italy to study the Tempa Rossa project, which is a much-hyped oil project in the Basilicata region of Italy. The company intends to study this integrated project for the technological aspects and the execution of the private investment.

Today, Shiva finds Sana exuding an infectious seduction. Her bangles jangle like cymbals calling for devotion, her shoulder-length hair has been let loose to waft stirringly in the slightest breeze and her eyes sparkle like they never have before. Her fragrance positively beckons, and Shiva comes to the conclusion that no cosmetic can bring as brilliant a shine to a woman as the hormones of happiness.

Throughout the day, he glances, as if compelled to, at Sana's tempting belly peeping above her sari, the bursting blossom of her breast cupped tightly under the blouse (the one not covered by the pallu) and the accentuation of the rounded buttocks below, letting his imagination take wing.

But Sana, unsure of the nature of Shiva's sudden thaw—or its duration—is careful not to let on anything that would bind her to the situation. She avoids looking long into his eyes, or staying long in his chamber. Plus, the thought of Shiva sensing the difference in her own demeanour makes her uneasy.

Shiva also finds the nature of Sana's new mellowness ambiguous, keeping him wondering if, having read his intentions in his tacit advances to her, she is equally reciprocating them. He has not been very forthright in matters of wooing women in spite of their innumerable attentions to him in his youth; he shied away as soon as his interaction with girls began turning amorous. But now his intended journey demands that he overpower his shyness.

The day is over. The vision of Akriti keeps blazing and diminishing in Shiva's mind depending upon how intensely Sana's glows; the two women remain nestled together in him, giving rise to a strange unease.

The rest of the week has been almost similar, and finally, the weekend arrives. This weekend for Shiva is hectic: gym, taking Ankur to the doctor for some final checks, bringing the boy's studies up to date to make up for the loss of school time, getting his own hair styled anew, spending some time with Akriti, completing official work at his laptop, and finally, to bed on Sunday night for his customary reading.

Tonight, he finishes a story about Lord Shiva abandoning his icy reserve to fall passionately in love with the heavenly sprite and temptress Mohini, and that too in front of his wife, Parvati. 'Even immovable God could not transcend nature, and turned adulterous,' he laughs at his own failing. His amusement grows when he recalls the great Rishi Vishwamitra, who had renounced his marital life for penance, but could not resist the seduction of the Apsara Menaka and even came to have a daughter by her, who was the famous Shakuntala, King Dushyant's beloved who gave birth to the illustrious King Bharata. It made him wonder how the taint of legitimacy did not succeed in tarnishing the greatness or even preventing the ascendancy of King Bharata to his rightful throne.

But even while reading, Shiva was distracted by painful visions of his wife in the arms of another man, leaving him to wonder how quickly tradition overthrows personal choice, and how challenging it is to live with intellect alone.

☒

# The Conquest of Sana

'Do you ever check your Whatsapp?' flashes on Shiva's mobile screen. It is from an unknown number. The display picture shows an attractive woman with a Panama hat atop flying tresses that blow around her face. She is wearing a pair of dark glasses embellished with some gold work on the frame, which lends considerable glamour to her picture. It is 10 in the night, and Shiva and Akriti have returned from their almost-silent stroll. Shiva, as his job demands, is going to sit at his laptop to check for the mails to update himself on the projects he's about to work on with the overseas clients. He is not able to make out who the woman in the picture is, but it gives him a thrill, anyway. Now and then, while still working, he casts a quick look at it, attempting to recognise Sana in it, but can't. In the excitement of the moment, he asks himself melodramatically, '*Is this the first milestone on my journey*?'

He retires to bed; since Ankur fractured his knee, Shiva has been sleeping alone in his son's room, and realises now that he prefers it that way. The prolonged proximity to Akriti had been growing emotionally hazardous.

'If it is an old friend, sorry for not recognising you. May I please know who this may be?' Shiva covertly sends the reply after some thought. He doesn't get a response, not even when he checks before leaving for the office next day.

'Sir, you have started looking younger and more energetic,' Prashant says a few days later, sitting in Shiva's chamber; he is there to discuss the Baku project of which he is the team leader. 'You have lost some weight, and the new hairstyle has made a world of difference.' The transformation of Shiva is dramatic enough to draw comments even from the reticent Prashant. Shiva instantly buoys up, recalling the intense admiration in Sana's eyes when she first saw him after he had had his hair styled anew; her eyes are testimony to the constant improvement in Shiva's appearance.

During the last few days, Shiva and Sana have been lavish with their compliments for each other, both vocally and sometimes with just a raised eyebrow and a rounded 'o' with their mouths, both expressive and coy. '*It's no one other than Sana*,' Shiva decides, '*who has sent the message*.'

'Yeah, I began feeling slothful of late. One has to watch one's weight in the forties,' says Shiva to other enquiring colleagues who have entered his room, turning away to hide his reddening face, wanting to squirm.

Just then, Sana enters his room with some letters and business magazines. 'Sir, I wanted to remind you of your visit to Mumbai on the coming Monday for the seminar. You have to finalise the presentation prepared by your team,' Sana says to Shiva.

'Yes, please check the presentation details with Rohit and let me know in an hour, because post-lunch I'll be busy briefing my core team on another project. By the way, what conference calls do I have today?'

'Let me check and get back to you, Sir.'

'Sure,' Shiva smiles and says, 'Don't worry too much; today is only Thursday, I am flying to Mumbai on Sunday.'

'But tomorrow you have a series of meetings, and I am on leave tomorrow...'

'I have that in mind, I can work at home on Saturday too if I need to.'

The day, as usual keeps Shiva busy with his presentation review, conference calls and interaction with his team.

As Shiva is wrapping up for the day, Sana says, 'By the way, Sir, you have begun looking boyish, and this navy-blue cod blazer is just fabulous.'

'Oh thanks, I also have something to say—I was so busy throughout the day I couldn't find the words or the time—you looked like a dark red flower today in that maroonish suit. It was quite a task focusing on my work.' Encouraged by Sana's compliments, Shiva was in full flow. The Whatsapp message gripped him yet again.

'Oh, thanks a lot, Sir. Somehow today I felt like dressing up. I'm really happy that you liked it,' Sana manages to say this through the gusts of glee that sweep over her. She adds, 'Please let me know if you need any assistance while you are in Mumbai.'

'Sure.' Shiva takes her 'I'm really happy that you liked it' as a step ahead in his conquest of Sana. In fact, he views the last as a foregone conclusion.

Finally they disperse, with hope in each of their hearts; they are not sure of anything yet, not even each other.

'Why did you get back so late today? I have been waiting for you since 6:30 pm,' Shiva, sounding irritated, asks the driver.

'Sir, I was with madam,' the driver says politely.

'Had you gone far?'

'Yes, sir, we had gone to Delhi, and you know, sir, how busy the Delhi-Gurgaon traffic is.'

Shiva falls silent. The letters spell out Akriti's name in flaming reds and golds again in his mind. '*If I am reconciled to Akriti seeing someone else*,' he asks himself complainingly, '*why am I still curious about her whereabouts? Perhaps this duel between "husband" and "man" will never end. He will win, eventually*.'

After getting home, Shiva is still plunged into sullenness; such days keep coming back despite his gritty resolution to live his life after the dictates of intellect rather than tradition. The disappointment from not getting any further message from the Whatsapp woman deepens his gloominess before he sleeps it off.

'Missing you' flashes on the mobile screen of Shiva the moment he enters his hotel room after the cocktail party. It is midnight, and Shiva is in Mumbai on a two-day trip for his seminar. It is again from the same number with the same display picture.

'Sana, missing you too,' Shiva decides to risk a full leap, flooded with euphoria brewed by the not-so-inconsiderable amount of scotch gone to his head. Somehow, Shiva is able to place Sana in the picture more confidently, thinking, 'Who else would miss me enough to send it? Only one of the two women I know well. It can't be Akriti, hence…'

The number has gone offline again; but as he descends into slumber, the mobile lights up with a blip, nudging him alert: 'Missing you, Sir.' This time Sana sends the message from her number, but instantly goes offline even before Shiva can reply.

Sana is feeling extremely shy. During the last few days the image of Shiva has given her life a glow, damping down any sense of guilt, keeping her body in a constant state of yearning. She has been struggling to restrain herself, thinking, 'I am a wife, and a mother, too. Falling for other man is a sin. Or isn't it?' The tug-of-war between desire and tradition isn't Shiva's alone. Sana is equally torn.

The new overwhelming chemistry between Shiva and her takes over and she ends up sending the messages, first discreetly, and tonight explicitly.

Shiva reciprocates with an 'Oh Sana!' The elation at his victory in winning over Sana, the sadistic excitement he derives from a vengeful ego, the anticipation of the much-awaited opportunity to study another marriage and the virtue of its female component, the sense of the bizarre in breaking out of tradition to follow an adulterous path—it also means going farther away from Akriti—the chance of feeding his starving passions! Shiva loses himself in a melee of delicious fantasies.

The following day passes without any message from Sana. By the day-end, Shiva grows impatient and messages her, 'Hi, Sana, how are you?' He doesn't want to let her go. He is flying back to Delhi tonight. No reply comes and he disappointedly puts his mobile in 'flight-mode' before the take-off of his Mumbai-Delhi flight. He remains restless during the two-hour journey. He reaches Delhi almost at midnight. As soon as he brings his mobile into network mode, he finds a long message darting in, but he doesn't read it, deciding to read it at leisure at home. He unlocks the door of his house and enters, taking care to not let

Akriti and Ankur hear his arrival, or disturb the help in the servant's room.

Shiva hurries to his bed, impatient to read Sana's message. It reads, 'Sorry for sending you all those messages. I was encouraged by your sudden dropping of reserves towards me and your warmth. My daughter arrived this morning for a short break. The sight of her gave me a pang of conscience for the guilt of falling for another man outside marriage. I felt contempt for myself, and the mere thought of her finding out almost killed me. What if the society gets to know? How shall I face anyone? Something else scares me; how can I let my husband touch my body while it is aching with desire for another man? I want to say much more, but all I can bring myself to say is that I'm sorry for causing you embarrassment. God knows how I will face you tomorrow. Please forgive me. Sana.'

The message leaves Shiva with a sense of loss. He can't bear to let Sana go. He manages to grab a few hours of sleep, then gives up trying for more. Then it's the usual gym, morning chores, and finally the office. Settling into his chair, Shiva grows conscious of the unease Sana's entry into his chamber will bring.

Instead, a calm and unruffled Sana walks in. 'Good morning sir, hope your presentation went well,' she says.

'Yes, thanks for all the support,' he replies in kind, though he is eyeing her keenly.

'Nothing major on your schedule for the day, Sir, except the dinner with the Iranian company at Crown Plaza. You have been invited with your spouse,' Sana's smile is the same politically correct 'office' smile, and that hurts him. She appears to be behaving the way she always did, not shying away from Shiva as he had been expecting her to.

'Thanks.' Shiva returns to brevity in speaking to her, looking coldly around the room. '*Not for nothing are women deemed to be the cleverer sex*,' he tells himself bitterly.

The two negotiate the day in a state of perpetual discomfiture. Sana makes her ritual winding-up-for-the-day entry in the evening. She looks the same, though inside she is scared of Shiva raking up what they went through during the last few days. But, he doesn't.

Almost a week passes without incident. Shiva's discomfiture worsens. Then it turns into desperation for Sana. '*I won her and lost her at once*,' he thinks, '*but at least I got her to admit she wants me, so my desirability stands proven. It is the guilt which overpowered her. How different she is from Akriti! But how thrilling it would be to totally win her over from her marriage! The possession of a woman can't be complete without attaining her body, and the prime focus of my quest is physical desire in marriage…*' Shiva is convinced of this while sleeping at night alone in his son's room; a 'distant togetherness' of Shiva and Akriti has now settled into a definite rhythm.

It is Sunday, and he has returned from a movie and dinner with his family. Ankur had been keen on an outing after the prolonged confinement to bed.

Shiva's thus-far silent mobile beeps.

'Thinking of you is driving me miserable,' Sana's message reads.

'Same here Sana. I feel I too have fallen for you. But why did you step back?'

Sana remains silent online for a while before messaging, 'I have already told you why, but now something weird is happening, which I can't even express.'

'Why? Please share it with me.'

'I can't, please don't insist, it is too strange a feeling to describe.'

'I think we should meet outside office where we can talk peacefully for some time; what say?' Shiva tries to advance aggressively.

'But… where?'

'Can we have lunch tomorrow? Anyway, we have to go out for the meeting.'

'You're taking me again to the meeting?'

'Yes, of course; attending meetings will expose you to new things and break the monotony of work as well; won't it be exciting to go club-dating along with the meeting?' Shiva says, teasingly.

The noisy duel between Shiva and her wifely duty causes Sana to pause before replying.

'So, tomorrow we are having lunch together for sure,' Shiva says with an air of finality.

'Goodnight.' Sana goes offline, not wanting to sound like she has weakened. She is already having trouble saying 'Shiva' instead of 'Sir'—even in her mind.

The conversation with Sana has left Shiva too excited to sleep. '*Did Akriti feel the same guilt when she stepped out with another man*?' he wonders, unable to stop making comparisons with his wife's infidelity.

'Yesterday you said something weird had happened to you,' Shiva asks Sana looking determinedly into her eyes; both of them are settled in a restaurant near their office for lunch.

'I am worried about being spotted with you alone by someone we know,' Sana says, looking around her nervously.

'Can't two colleagues have an occasional lunch out?' Shiva is a bit taken aback, reflecting, '*Working in the corporate sector and yet so orthodox*!'

Seeing her still uncomfortable, Shiva calms her down. 'Don't worry, the office knows you have come out for an official meeting.'

Sana remains jittery. Shiva has already ordered the food, having somehow managed to force her choice out of her.

'Sana, we don't have much time, not even in our whole lives. Life is too short to waste on fretting and worrying. You had been swimming against the tide thus far, so why not have a go at swimming along with it?'

'Swimming against the tide?'

'Yes, Sana, I can sense you are not happy in… anyway, forget it, and explain what you meant yesterday by "weird".'

'It's just that it's never happened before,' she says, looking confused. 'I resisted you so strongly, and now I desire you just as much.' Sana pauses for a while, her lips quivering, and continues, 'I am getting drenched with desire.'

'That is something to relish, not worry about. Your body found freedom from the prison of your mind to seek refuge in your heart. And do you know why that has not happened earlier?' Shiva asks. Sana is silent, discomfited by the revelation she has just made to Shiva.

'The heart is the most precious organ in the body,' Shiva persists, 'but ironically, the most neglected as well. Aren't we compelled to live by our minds mostly?' Shiva turns conscious of his transition from the glib to the profound. 'I sincerely believe in what I just said,' Shiva feels comforted by this assertion.

Sana thinks for a while and says, 'Men won't understand. I am a woman. Being unfaithful is bound to induce a stronger guilt in my sex. Society expects women to be more moral. I told you how the sight of my daughter made me feel less of a mother. As a wife too it will be difficult for me to manage…' Sana pauses momentarily before saying, 'I have already shared my feelings.'

'As a wife it will be difficult for you to manage what?' Shiva repeats her earlier words, 'What do you mean, Sana?'

Shiva drops pebbles into Sana to bring up the poison in her to the fore, 'I would not be able to handle the kind of physical passion I feel for you, which is enough for me to melt. I wanted to feel the same way for my husband, but he left me dry. But still I had to… I feel if I step out further, even doing that would be difficult.'

'Should I take "dry" to mean forced sex?'

Sana hesitates before finally crying out softly, 'I was only twenty when I was married off. No one bothered to seek my consent to the match. I had never fallen seriously in love with any boy before marriage. But, somewhere deep down in my heart, I wanted my husband to be the man of my dreams: handsome and tall and broad-shouldered, especially since I was raised to believe I was a very beautiful girl. My heart hankered for a suitable match. But as is the wont of women, I reined in my cravings and entered the marriage with a sense of complete commitment. Somehow, he could never succeed in making sex a pleasurable experience.' She paused and took a long breath.

'Then pregnancy was imposed upon me—hardly within a year of my marriage. When my baby arrived, it was so difficult to know how to manage, given my own tender age. When I took up working, things became worse. My mother-in-law never lent a supporting hand. On the contrary, I remained under the constant pressure to prove myself a dutiful daughter-in-law. My mother-in-law kept finding fault in me, and under her provocation, my husband kept yelling at me—and occasionally went to the extent of hitting me, too. I can't forget one instance—the mere memory of it makes me sick. That changed everything… for ever.' Sana feels too agitated to talk further, her voice sinking, her face contorted.

'What was it? Come on, it's important to have someone in your life on whom you can unburden your heart, or you'll break with grief.' Shiva tries to convince her to follow her heart with liberal doses of philosophy.

Sana relents and opens up. 'My younger sister had come to meet me during the days of my pregnancy. In a playful moment with her I stumbled and fell. Hearing me fall, he rushed in from the next room and slapped my face hard. I froze out of shock. This humiliation, that too in front of my sister, enraged me. He was worried about the child in my womb coming to any harm because of my fall, not the woman who was to bear the child. Something snapped in my mind, echoing the sound of that violent slap. Since then I have been just a mother living with the father of my daughter, so that she is not deprived of paternal security,' Sana's withheld sorrow burst its dam, engulfing her voice.

'Then what makes you feel so guilty?' Shiva's hopes rise, with this disclosure of a brutal husband.

'Because adultery is a sin,' she whispers, her head bent.

'What makes you think so?'

'Once, my mother-in-law organised the traditional ritual when I was pregnant. Sacred scriptures were recited; the priest said that it was written in the Puranas that if anyone indulged in adultery, after death they would be stuck to a red-hot metal effigy of themselves. The mere thought of it drove shivers down my spine, and that image stayed in my mind.'

Shiva instantly breaks into a mocking smile, before saying, 'By the way, who came back from heaven, sorry, hell, to share this experience?'

'Are you making fun of me?'

'Do you believe in what these scriptures say?' asks Shiva in turn.

'Of course; they are the books of wisdom teaching man the norms of conduct.'

'Have you read them yourself, from end to end?' Shiva smiles sardonically.

'There are too many and too vast. I know only what elders keep referring to; otherwise I am not keen on finding out much.'

'Fine. And now tell me, what remains of man after death?'

'His soul.'

'Weapons cleave it not, fire burns it not, water moistens it not, wind dries it not?' Shiva suppresses a smile.

'Now, what is that?' Sana looks bemused.

'That is is what the Gita says about the soul—and I need not add that it is held to be the essence of Hindu philosophy. So, how can one burn what can't be burnt?' Shiva takes a self-satisfied gulp of coke.

'You are trying to confuse me.' This time, it is Sana who suppresses a smile, disguising the action by taking a spoonful of her paneer tikka. 'So now, you are a priest, too, reciting the scriptures and all.'

'When they are so many, and at variance with each other, you have to be your own priest,' Shiva says, surprisingly pleased with his own profundity.

Sana slips into a thoughtful pause.

Shiva says, encouraged by his words apparently working well on her, 'You said those words of wisdom dictate the norms of conduct?'

'Yes, otherwise Ahilya would not be turned into a stone by her husband, Sage Gautam, because of her adulterous relationship with God Indra.'

Shiva laughs out loud. 'Thank God such miracle-working sage-husbands don't exist these days!'

'Are you making fun of me again?'

'Not at all. But let me give you examples in the scriptures of the affairs of gods, let alone man.'

'You will cite the instance of Lord Shiva falling for Mohini, and that too in the presence of his wife Parvati,' Sana intercepts him smugly.

'That is one, and he is nevertheless held to be the supreme God by many Hindus. But I wanted to tell you about the adultery of Lord Brihaspati, as He is held to be the God of wisdom in Hindu tradition, and you just described these scriptures as "books of wisdom",' Shiva says, refusing to be halted in mid-speech.

'Okey… ' Sana sounds curious.

'Lord Brihaspati, in his weaker moments, lusted after Mamata, the wife of his brother, Uthaya, and made love to her although she was pregnant by her husband at the time. And we continue to regard him as a god!'

'But he was male, and males are known to behave that way.'

'Come on, Sana, it's not the God but godliness that matters. And you yourself said a little while ago that anyone who commits adultery is treated the same in the Puranas, regardless of gender. They don't differentiate between a man and woman,' Shiva sniggers.

'I don't know all that but I know it is different for a woman.'

'Does that mean you would tolerate your husband turning adulterer?'

Sana is taken aback, falling silent, her conviction weakened. She stops eating, though still looking down, her expression an implicit acceptance of what Shiva has told her. She wonders how she could have revealed—without actually saying it—to an outsider that her husband had sex with other women when he was on his business tours. Shiva, in his turn, wonders, '*A financially independent woman silently bearing not only the cruelty of her husband, but his adultery too?*'

Breaking the difficult silence, Shiva goes on to tease her further, 'Well, now let me narrate the adventure of a demigoddess. Have you heard the story of Tara?'

'I am not sure; but why...'

'Please be patient for just a little longer,' Shiva interrupts her. 'I just want to illustrate how the scriptures don't always agree with each other—which is why it's such a tricky business to come to a moral conclusion on many matters in life.'

'Okay, then.'

'Thanks. Now it's the turn of the wife of Lord Brihaspati. Tara, bored with the lifestyle of her husband who was immersed in knowledge and rituals, grew attracted to Chandra, the moon god, who was intensely passionate and a crafty lover. Believing that in him she would find what she really wanted in life, she eloped with Chandra.

Brihaspati was both sad and angry, but he needed

Tara to conduct the rituals he engaged in to strengthen the Devas, or gods, against the Asuras, or demons. Such rituals, you see, demanded the presence of a wife. He tried to persuade Tara to come back, but she refused. Brihaspati pleaded with the other gods to help him get her back. It was finally Lord Indra, the patron of Brihaspati, who directed Tara to return to her husband in order that the rituals continue apace.' Shiva looks at Sana for a reaction.

'Are you sure Tara went unpunished?'

'Her husband cursed her womb, and hence her son by Chandra was born blind.'

'That's what…'

'Tell me honestly, even talking in mythological terms, do you agree that an adulterous husband can remain godly enough for perpetrating such curses?' Shiva smiles mischievously.

'Have you done a thesis on the adultery of gods?' Sana asks wryly.

'Of the gods made by man; not the God who made man.' Profundity again sets Shiva aglow.

'What do you want to prove? That adultery is not deviance from sacred laws?'

'I believe that both deviance and observance are the directions in which your inner voice guides you. I feel you fell for me because of your unfulfilled desires and your husband's brutish behaviour. And, in any case, desire weakens after a certain time in marriage. Tara wanted passion, so she went to Chandra, refusing to bear the deprivation of it. I believe that it is man who has written all these stories, and made the gods behave in human ways, realising that the perfect examples of fidelity that Rama and Sita embodied could always be not emulated.' Shiva is, by now, gesticulating, taking delight in his oratory, determined to convince Sana that all he says is true.

'Do you mean to say that we should violate the sacrament of marriage to fulfil our wilder desires?'

'"Violating" doesn't mean breaking out of marriage. You have just learnt how both Brihaspati and Tara fulfilled their desires outside marriage and yet continued living together, for pragmatic reasons, although they knew of each other's infidelities. This story truly dispenses wisdom. You too are continuing in marriage not as a wife but as a responsible mother. I feel, unless it becomes unbearable, one should continue the marriage.' Shiva puts on a wistful expression, hoping he's getting through to Sana. He keenly assesses Sana's mood before continuing, 'Of course, the final choice is yours, whether you want to follow the social rules out of irrational fear, treating them as sacrosanct even when they don't bring you peace, or deviate a little to get some happiness. But yes, complete secrecy is certainly important to avoid trouble of any kind—we can't all be like Brihaspati and Tara and carry on like nothing happened, after one of a couple has had an affair.'

'It's not that these thoughts didn't cross my mind,' Sana admits, 'but yet the guilt stays put'.

'Why guilt—in your case? Is the sex forced on you by your husband not marital rape? And yet our social rules dictate that sex be confined to marriage. Logically, does it not mean legalising rape? Law is now waking up to these murky realities. I hold that guilt arises from a malfunction of conscience, not from breaking meaningless social norms.'

'Life can be so complex!' sighs Sana.

'Yes it is, but not so much in your case. If you loved your husband, that could have overpowered the other issues including the unsatisfactory sex, but you don't, so no guilt, please,' Shiva stops for a fleeting second, and then continues as persuasively as he can, 'You can't live a happy life without a little deviance and a few lies; do you want me to tell you another story to establish it?' Mischief sparkles again in Shiva's eyes.

'Are you too missing something in life?' Sana cuts him off, her own face solemn.

'That is obvious,' Shiva says vaguely.

Sana appears to be hypnotised by Shiva, oblivious to time. They have been in the restaurant for more than two hours.

Watching her relax now, his conquest of Sana by now assured, Shiva acknowledges to himself that he, too, is in the zero time zone. His engineering days pop up, reminding him of the concept of 'time dilation', which implies spending more time with the sense of spending less.

Suddenly, Sana's hands move to cover his on the table. Shiva has been anticipating this, but her touch confirms his victory.

'Anything else, Sir? We are closing now for the evening,' the waiter breaks their enchanted spell.

'Oh! It is so late?' Sana says looking at her watch.

Both of them leave for the office. On the way back, Sana feels overwhelmed by the rush of her emotions. Office, home, family—all are a distant blur. She manages the remaining time at work almost like an automaton till it's time to do her ritual winding-up in Shiva's chamber.

'I'm leaving,' Sana says feebly.

Shiva finds her not addressing him as 'Sir' novel and exciting. He smiles into her eyes without speaking, not wanting to break the rhythm of this delightful unease.

Sana's exit turns Shiva reflective about their meeting in the restaurant. '*Was I being a sophist,*' he asks himself, '*using my idea of logic to get her to fall in with my scheme? I think not. I guided her towards what I genuinely believe is true about the separate concepts of marriage and desire. And it was she who made the first advance. She looked so happy to be with me, body and mind. Dharma can't dictate such an utter deprivation of happiness.*'

Truth, reason, desire, marriage, extra-marital relationships, the good, the bad—all mix into a nebulous haze in his mind. He rises in a hurry to lose himself in the mundane motions of life. Nothing urgent at hand, he winds up to leave for home.

It has been almost a week since they met in the restaurant. They have now melded almost completely with each other's minds. Their early formality in his chamber has changed to passionate gazes, amorous and stealthy holding of hands, and brushing against each other whenever they find themselves in proximity. They yearn for a chance of seclusion to spill their brimming passions, which will ultimately demolish the traditional boundaries..

Akriti, on the other hand, has receded into a dim recess of Shiva's mind. Whenever home, Shiva and Sana get into extended chats with each other. Shiva is not much bothered about Akriti observing his sudden attachment to his mobile. On the contrary, he vindictively wishes that she would, viewing his changed behaviour, discover his liaison with another woman.

'The project report is almost ready, Sir.' Prashant briefs Shiva on the company's ambitious project in Baku. 'I will furnish the draft to you by this afternoon. The MD wants to have a discussion on it with us next week. After that we can directly freeze the deal with the other investors. All of them have nearly agreed.'

Shiva gathers his thoughts to focus on what Prashant is saying. Sana, sitting next to him, snatches all his attention, silently, gleefully.

Shiva nods a general 'Fine' to Prashant.

'With the finalisation of the Detailed Project Report, you should begin planning your visit to Baku, and Italy, too, to study the Tempa Rossa project,' Sana puts in.

'By the day-end, I shall finish reading the report and freeze it. I have a tight schedule tomorrow, so do try to submit it by lunchtime,' Shiva says to Prashant.

'I will do my best, Sir. The draft is more-or-less ready; I only have to check it once more.'

'Wonderful, may I request you, Sana, to stay back a bit in the evening?' Shiva's smile into Sana's eyes assumes a deceitful hue; she relishes the surety in their mutual attraction.

'Certainly, Sir,' she returns, trying to sound nonchalant in Prashant's presence, the sinful sparkle in her eyes still there.

'Sana has always been known for her devotion to duty,' Prashant says, turning to the door.

Shiva is rushing through the report, trying to stop his attention from straying to Sana. She has been either around or moving in and out, tackling some work or the other, including organising the folder for another international seminar next week. It is almost 7 in the evening. Sana's footsteps, returning to his door after yet another errand outside, echo in the emptying hall beyond his chamber. He becomes acutely conscious of their approaching moment of privacy. She enters the room. Shiva feigns reading the last pages of the report when Sana comes around the desk and stands close to him.

'Is it still not over?' she asks peeking at the report. 'No problem, take your time.' The rustle of Sana's outfit brushing against Shiva's shoulders lends their time together a thrilling expectancy.

'I'm almost through.'

Shiva reclines, removing his reading glasses and letting his head rest on the back of the chair. He presses his eyes to convey his weariness, inviting Sana's tender response. Sana strokes his hair, saying, 'Shall I make some coffee for you? The office boy has left.' The touch of Sana's hand triggers his passions. Turning towards her, he takes her into his embrace, cupping her Rubenesque buttocks with his palms, and burying his head in her belly; Shiva is revelling in the fantastic fleshy opulence. She draws Shiva in to convey her surrender. She bends over him and Shiva's head now looks for her heaving breasts. '*Breasts are truly the speakers of a woman's heart*', he thinks. Rising from his chair, he kisses all over her face and neck, his hands travelling all over her body. Desire drenches Sana again; the aroma of it permeates Shiva's nostrils, making him dizzy. They are painfully conscious that they can't go beyond this in the chamber, and force themselves apart, Sana rearranging her ruffled clothes; they are raging seas seeking the shores for some relief. The room goes eerily silent.

'I will wrap up the report at home,' Shiva resorts to speech to calm himself.

'Yes, I'm getting late. It's almost dark outside.' It is a summer evening, and the delayed sunset comforts some of the anxiety dusk brings to Sana.

'I hope you've informed your people at home that you'd be late?' Shiva asks Sana politely.

'Whom would I inform? My husband is out on tour.' Sana's words at once release the raging bull in Shiva out of its fragile pen. No matter how hard he tries to disguise the fact, she knows it.

'I was going to drop you home, anyway,' Shiva tries to look casual, even indifferent, secretly relishing the suggestion of a shy invitation in Sana's eyes.

Shiva takes the car keys from his desk; he has already let his driver off, and they set out together. During the drive, they chat like co-passengers. 'It was a tiring day,' Shiva says, his mind fixed upon the moment when he will have to drop Sana off at her lonely home. They are about to get there.

'Yes, you need some good coffee and some rest.' Coffee has come to symbolise Sana's tender care which never fails to stir Shiva; her care fulfils what remains unfulfilled at home. The currents of life are truly conducted through their contrasts.

'Yes, I do.' Shiva's heart beats hard in anticipation of an invitation.

'By the way, I make better coffee at home than you get at the office. Want to try some?' Sana asks, smiling coyly over her shoulder while getting down from the car.

'But won't it be a bit tiring for you after a day's slog?' Shiva's tone conveys his tacit acceptance.

'I'll be making it for myself anyway.' Shiva notices the anticipation lighting her face.

Sana directs him to the lift which takes them to her floor, and lets herself into her house, ushering him in, her heart pounding. She makes Shiva comfortable on the sofa of her living room and goes into the kitchen to brew the coffee. Shiva's eyes fall upon a photo frame on the wall; it is a family photograph of Sana with her husband and daughter; the mismatch between Sana's and her husband's looks strikes him. He sweeps his gaze around the house, aware that he is in another man's territory.

'Freshen up if you like. You'll feel better,' Sana says, entering the living room carrying a tray.

'Okay, I'll do just that.'

Sana guides him to the washroom.

'If you don't mind, could I change quickly?' she asks from behind him.

'Sure, by all means.'

While washing his face and hands, Shiva reflects, '*How difficult it is to face Sana with no one else around! Despite my resolve to have her, why am I feeling so hesitant? How apart is thinking from doing!*'

Shiva comes out from the washroom and settles back into the sofa. Sana comes in, having changed into a Patiala suit. Shiva has never seen her in a salwar suit before. It has sculpted her fulsome figure perfectly, accentuating the novelty of her new look to him. While walking to the sofa, Sana loosens her hair from its sleek chignon, letting it uncoil silkily down her back, and tosses her head. Shiva believes a woman untying her hair in the presence of a man is directly leading him on.

Both get talking, exchanging the generalities, like their usual routine in the evenings with their family, and so on. Shiva's eyes inadvertently revert to the family photograph. Sana's gaze follows his.

'So, that's your husband…'

Shiva can see the darkness dimming the glow in her eyes, and feels guilty. A sensitive and trustworthy man should help a woman forget, not remember, her sadness.

'I was treated very badly for bringing an insufficient dowry to the marriage; the scars haven't healed, nor will they ever,' Sana says, her eyes now glistening with tears.

'No tears, okay? Why can't you draw comfort from the fact that you are not the only woman facing all this?' Shiva leans forward and clasps her hands between both of his consolingly.

Shiva's tender touch instantly drives her molten, and she draws him into her hungry arms. Shiva caresses her hair to convey the surge of his affection, with their passion already gaining surety. Silence takes over, hushing their loud passionate cries into gasps and whispers of long-denied lust. They remain there till, as if by unspoken agreement, they head to the bedroom, still locked in each other's arms, uncaring of everything around, and collapse on the bed. Here, they give their desperate bodies a full rein. The room is dimly lit by the bedside lamps, wrapped in a sensuous translucence, it is a sumptuous stage for the lovers' first full-bodied tryst. They keep rummaging each other for a wild while, their hands and mouths impatiently seeking each other all over. Shiva craves to attain Sana in all her bare softness, his hands frenziedly sweeping up and down the dips and rises of her body, lingering longer on the rises. Ultimately he takes charge of her. His eyes fall upon a framed photo on the side table showing Sana with her husband. He softly turns the picture on its face, lest it arouse her feelings of guilt again. But she hears the clink of the frame, and lifting her benumbed self, stretches out her hand to right it. No later, she rides him furiously. Shiva instantly knows what is happening: her passion has taken on the colour of revenge, and she wants her husband to 'see' her pent-up desires released for the first time. He, too, derives an unusual pleasure in the act of her 'punishing' the man who is not there to witness their animal love in reality. In no time, Sana is rhythmically working hard upon him, trying to suck everything out of him with an unrelenting fury, with Shiva's hands indecisively shuttling between her breasts and her fetishistic Rubenesque buttocks, gorging on their lushness. Together they foment a complete fantasy, mingling their juices freely and with thirst.

The shrieks of Sana-the-seductress now bring Shiva into full action. He is still far from climaxing. His passion is a furious mix of hunger long unsated, and an arrogant urge to prove his own desirability. Added to this is the animal thrill in winning over a woman from her previous mate. Sana is writhing on the bed, tossing and turning frenziedly, offering every inch of her neglected body to his enchanting touch. They feel so completely taken up at each and every step that the climax is deferred time and again, neither wanting the arrival at the destination that will mean an end to this indescribable journey. Now, Shiva begins to buck and rear, she arches towards him, and they finally spend themselves in a mutual, blissful outpouring.

They lie there weary but content, their fingers trailing lazy patterns on each other's bodies.

Shiva lying replete on the bed, reflects, '*Oh, what have I been missing*!'

Sana pulls the bunched-up counterpane over their cooling bodies with a sigh. Shiva senses the guilt returning to her. A woman's superego is nothing less than a glacier and its meltdown is bound to carry the rubble of guilt.

'Do you regret this?' Shiva asks her.

'I don't want to, but …' Sana slips into reflection.

'Sana, I know, in spite of all the logic in the world, guilt refuses to die. Even a curative surgery leaves a scar. But don't you think it is the very sense of sin which lent thrill to what we tasted just now? Just imagine how boring would be the sight of the sea kissing the shore without any surf washing over? So treat this guilt as the cost of bliss. Nothing in life comes free.' Shiva is at his sophisticated best.

'You sound so convinced and look so calm! Is there any issue in your marriage as well?' Sana persists for the second time. 'You said in the restaurant that you are missing something.'

'I too am living a typical marriage.'

'Ok-a-y...' Sana senses his hesitance in telling her more, thinking, '*Men don't speak at length like we women do. I told him everything in detail, but he conveyed his all in one sentence*.'

'Life doesn't provide a total solution. Guilt is still needling me,' Sana says pensively, while rising from the bed. She dresses herself, preparing to get him something to eat.

'But your inner voice prevailed over guilt. Some issues are very complex, Sana. You yourself have to deduce the truth with reason on such issues, if at all it exists.' Shiva speaks from his heart, unadulterated with any other intention this time.

'It's impossible to resist you. Your logic and your words win me over each time,' Sana admits. 'But, how do you know so much about myths and legends?' Sana looks at him, her eyes alive with fondness, then turns to go into the kitchen. Shiva, too, is getting dressed.

'When I feel any anxiety over digressing from the trodden path,' says Shiva, calmly buttoning his shirt, 'I read up on stories in which the man-made gods conducted themselves, in ways not always recommended,' says Shiva smugly. 'Otherwise,' he raises his voice so she can hear him from the kitchen, 'how could I have cracked a hard nut like you?'

'Who would have thought such a decent-looking guy would have been such a smooth-talking flirt!'

'Oh, damn!' says Shiva, looking at his watch. 'I have to leave, although it doesn't feel like I've spent a lot of time here.'

'But I've brought some cake and nuts for you,' Sana protests. 'Here, have some.'

'Thanks, but I'm really late for dinner. The time flew by so quickly.' Shiva turns conscious of the zero time zone again.

Sana pushes a piece of cake into his mouth; Shiva kisses her and makes his exit.

While leaving, Shiva's emotions are a strange mix of bliss from satiation of passions long denied, a thrilling sense of victory in winning over Sana with his intellectual sophistication, a sadistic pleasure out of an indirect revenge against Akriti, an affectionate tenderness for Sana, and a strange pang from severance from Akriti getting wider. And by the time he enters his car, he is assailed by the growing feeling that he is using Sana and truth to a sinister end.

⊠

# Resurrection of Deven

Loving truth is far from living it. If Shiva has been able to establish the truth behind what he and Sana are up to, why is he still tormented by the confusion he has carried in his mind from Sana's? Right-wrong, contentment-discontentment…all lie in an inextricable mix. Is this mix the truth? They say truth is beautiful. But they also say truth is bitter. Then what is the real feel of truth?

'You're so late, is everything all right?' Akriti says as Shiva sits on the sofa, removing his shoes.

'Great. So you're finally concerned with what happens to me,' Shiva says wrily.

'At times office work holds you back, so I thought…'

'If you know that, why ask now?'

'It's much later than even on your busiest day.'

The hint of puzzlement over Shiva's unusual lateness is only half noticeable in Akriti's tone, but Shiva finds it gratifying anyway.

'It never bothered you before… but forget it.' Though Shiva is by now accustomed to Akriti's indifference to his presence or absence, the old bitterness persists. Reality doesn't change, but the response does.

Akriti, realising that Shiva is upset, decides to bring in dinner and carry on with the rest of their 'routine' to calm his mood. Later, Shiva retires to bed after 'cuddle time' with Ankur, the proximity to his son's tender, innocent body soothing his troubled heart.

Appeased somewhat, he goes back to his mobile to chat with Sana. Akriti's unquestioning acceptance of his sudden attachment to his mobile bothers him. '*Wouldn't my revenge be doubled if Akriti came to know of my affair*?'

'*Oh, what is this black hole I sense in my mind*!' Shiva struggles to sleep. '*A black hole is a region of space having a gravitational field so intense that no matter or radiation can escape from it.*' The words of the physics professor of his engineering college ring in his mind. Like a black hole, the gravity of his mind has become so intense that no thought escapes from it, and thus it can't radiate the hue of any particular emotion. His thoughts are too convoluted to throw up any truth. He feels tormented by keeping them inside himself; he craves for someone with whom he can share it all. The name Deven springs to his mind at once, adding nostalgia to confusion. With no one around, wearied of groping to identify the black hole within him, he falls asleep; the path to the soul is dark, lonely and frightening.

Shiva reaches his office in the morning to collect the material for his seminar and pass the instructions for the day's business; the seminar is at a hotel in Delhi. He meets Sana who exudes a breezy vivacity. Both find each other glowing from the effects of their last encounter. But such joys leave one hankering for more; their passions are on the prowl again. They decide to meet in the evening as Sana's husband is returning the next day. Shiva stops for a while before leaving his chamber, checks the door, and plants a quick kiss on her blushing cheek.

While Shiva is driven to the hotel where the seminar is to be held, the black hole deepens, making his need for a confidant all the more urgent. He decides he must get in touch with Deven. Tomorrow will be Saturday, he will have time to ascertain Deven's whereabouts. After their student years were over, they remained in touch for some time before the pace of living compelled them to lose sight of each other. They last met a little after Shiva's wedding, when Deven was struggling to set up his business venture. Last heard, he was looking for fresh prospects after the farming project at his native place in UP failed to take off.

Shiva gathers himself for the last session of the seminar before lunch, which is on the 'Global Oil Scenario'. As the day's end approaches, his only thought is of meeting Sana again.

Shiva reaches Sana's house. She greets him with a passionate kiss. She is wearing a sexy satin gown. Shiva instantly clasps her tightly, and kisses her deeply on her mouth. Just one encounter, and they already know each other's bodies, and how best to moisten their parched selves. They hasten directly to the bedroom and make frenzied love.

Later, Shiva sits up against the pillows, in a mood of mellow but intense togetherness, sipping wine and looking down and caressing Sana's hair while she lays with her head in his lap.

Sana suddenly looks grave.

'What's the matter?' Shiva asks worriedly.

'I wonder, you said that desire doesn't last in marriage. It sounded correct, but then marriage must have been created with more lasting meaning…' Sana falls silent.

'I know what's troubling you. Let me narrate an anecdote to you I read recently. Shvetaketu, an ancient sage, grew very disturbed when he found that his father Uddalaka was displeased by the amorous associations of his wife with the other sages. He decided to frame the law of marriage so that men could know who their fathers were. As far as I know, the need for marriage was felt to record official progeniture, so that a family could be defined in terms of father, mother and children, and it could function as a fundamental unit of society. In addition, marriages have taken place out of economic and political reasons too, even in ancient times—you must have heard the legends about how and why gods and kings married. Lord Krishna used marriage for strategic reasons—to expand his empire—and out of compassion, too, to lift the gopis out of social ignominy. Desire, per se, what you call kama, was never the centre of marriage.'

'You have an answer to every question,' Sana pouts.

'To retain one's sanity, one has to invent the answers to the tricky questions life keeps throwing up,' Shiva retorts. 'And yes, I have discovered something else in your scriptures which can take care of your guilt,' Shiva says, turning a bit naughty.

'*My* scriptures? Still making fun of me? Anyway, what is your great discovery?'

'It's a *smriti*; it says that a woman can have sex with another man if her husband has deserted her; I believe being emotionally deserted means as much.'

'You and your logic...' Sana says half-dismissively.

'Shall I ask you something, if you don't mind?' Shiva is still stroking her hair while he sips his wine.

Sana silently nods.

'After marriage, did you ever feel attracted to someone else before me?'

The flush of fulfilled desire on Sana's face instantly pales. She stays quietly sad for a minute or two before saying, 'So now you are growing suspicious, thinking, if I have fallen for you I might have fallen for someone else too?'

'Not at all, Sana; please don't mistake my meaning.'

'Then, like a typical man, you have turned inquisitive about my past,' Sana is unrelenting.

'Please…in that case, let me correct my question. What made you fall for me and not anyone else before? I mean, you have been working with other men—bosses, colleagues—was there never any attraction on either side? I'm just trying to understand you better as a friend.' Shiva injects all the politeness at his command into his words to prevent offending her. He is trying, as he'd planned to, to understand the mind of a married woman.

'When you first came into the office, I found you to be decent and reserved; you never ogled me, and that felt good for a change. Later, when you began being friendly, I thought it was out of a genuine liking for me, the person, not the woman. And when you softened even more, I came to relish your advances and grew increasingly attracted to you. And yes, when I sensed that you appreciated every gesture I made showing care, the typical concern of a personal secretary began changing into the tender care of a loving woman. But you still didn't exhibit any sign of hurry, nor did you force your attentions on me. I found you to be a man who approaches a woman through her heart, not her body. And of course, your reasoned arguments convinced me that I was not committing any sin. Beyond this, I have already told you all, about my marriage, my past…' Sana stops mid-sentence and abruptly rises from his lap, turns towards him, and says, 'and I like a man tall and broad enough to provide a woman a man-sized embrace.' A slight giggle escapes her. Shiva holds her tight against him.

'Now I feel tempted to ask you something,' says Sana.

'Feel free.'

'I frequently sense an emptiness in you. Are you not happy? Yesterday you avoided answering that question.' Sana is at her inviting best, taking a sip from his glass.

'I have a typical marriage; years of coexistence have taken away the novelty. There have been areas of incompatibility, and sometimes the weight of responsibilities takes their toll. Topping it all, there is a femme fatale in my office who can rob even a devout puritan of all his morals.' Suddenly, Shiva finds himself at his most seductive.

He doesn't reveal that his wife's adultery has placed him on a path strewn with many women, of whom she is one.

'I really never anticipated that this seemingly reserved man could be so romantic!' Sana kisses him again.

After chatting for a while about their budding relationship and making plans for future meetings, Shiva finally leaves her house.

Moments lived are not moments dead; they can vivify themselves and come back to sit right before you, as if the journey was never broken.

'Ah! It feels as if it was just yesterday,' Shiva erupts into a boyish exuberance.

'Time doesn't always fly by, it can fly back too,' nostalgia turns Deven equally exuberant.

'Don't you think that it is not always that time is more powerful than man? See how our meeting again has brought back the past?'

'Time,' agrees Shiva, 'can neither define nor measure itself without man. Only man can make sense of time.' They feel like they've never been separated by years or circumstances. 'So, back in our element right away, huh? It's like we're still chatting in a corner of the college campus.'

'Yes, and has time not returned us to our youth?'

'*You* certainly are the same—tall and "socialist-thin".' In their early ears, this is how Shiva used to describe his skeletal friend.

'*You've* put on weight, but it suits you. Also, the thick hair, that attracted girls so much, has thinned a bit,' Deven says.

The two are chatting in a beer café, finally together again. It is a Sunday, almost a fortnight since Shiva decided to work on tracking Deven down. The alumni list of DCE (Delhi College of Engineering) finally helped him find his friend. Deven lives in Mumbai now, having set up a flourishing export company there.

Their friendship is kind of the coming-together of opposites; it was only their fascination for the otherworldly which was common to them. Deven's personality is an interesting blend of contradictions. On the one hand, being a poet, he loves talking and writing about the matters of the heart, soul and fate. On the other, he pursues business as a way to make quick money, in order to fund his political ambitions. 'A socialistic body, a poetic heart, and a capitalistic head' is how Shiva also used to describe him.

Shiva used to be a keen debater in those days, and remained an avid reader of history and mythology. By now, his reading has sharpened his appetite for looking for logic in all things, and integration in man. Deven, however, revels in the dichotomy in man, which once prompted him to allude to Gandhi as being a sublime saint and a master strategist at the same time.

Deven has told Shiva his plans to enter the catering business in Delhi; he is trying to take on lease a prime property of a hotel in which to operate a restaurant.

'What is the progress so far?' Shiva asks eagerly, pleased that his childhood friend would soon be frequenting his city.

'It's well on track, but it was a pain resolving a major obstacle on the way.'

'What was that?'

'Well, the tender for this property was not being put out because the previous holder cooked up a legal wrangle as he didn't want to pay off his dues. Hence, the matter became sub judice. We were confident that we would get the contract as we had already decided to submit a very high quote; you have to bear some loss initially to make big money in the future,' Deven says typically.

'And then?' Shiva prompts him with a wicked grin.

'I had to seek the help of a senior IPS colleague of my brother to get him in line. You know, *asuras* listen to only *dand* and *danda*—demons can only be beaten into obedience.' Shiva is reminded more and more of the young Deven.

'It sounds too simple. Anyway, you must have enjoyed solving the problem in the way you know best.' Shiva is beginning to slur his words, the second beer having gone quickly to his head.

Deven notices an unmistakable look of sadness in Shiva's eyes. He can sense the youthful exuberance in Shiva fading fast. Shiva tells him first about his job, his rise to the present coveted position, but confesses that the kick he got out of this rise has been pretty short-lived, a sense of ennui settling in.

'That's nothing abnormal—a typical midlife syndrome. What about your family?' Shiva lifts his half-filled mug and downs the beer in one go. Then all his pent-up experiences pour out of him—his marital life or lack of it, his journey of discovery, and Sana. He also reveals the black hole in his mind.

Deven is stirred to sympathy but tries to cheer up Shiva. 'Buddy, so you are enjoying screwing a sexy woman, so what?'

A faint smile flits over Shiva's now sad face. Deven goes on, 'Brother, make merry. Your debating skills have paid off. They've persuaded a staid married woman into your bed, so why rue it?'

'But this black hole in my mind just refuses to change its colour,' Shiva continues depressed.

'Recall, you used to say that discovering truth is like traversing a tunnel, mesmerised by the light at the end. This light, this truth, goes out in marriage, but adultery comes in to help you find your way. Some years from now people will laud you for it. "Shiva establishes the value of adultery" they will shout from the rooftops.' Deven erupts into hushed cheers.

'Knowing truth is a pleasure, but living it can be such a pain!'

'Enough of it; your journey involves screwing many other women you want to conquer, and tasting the excitement of a guilt-free desire. God give that good fortune to all!'

'My desire is not guilt-free, Deven; if it was, then this black hole wouldn't be there.'

'I understand. Our superego doesn't dissolve that quickly; Akriti will keep rankling you either way.'

'Now I feel attached to Sana. Anyway, do you approve of the reason for taking revenge on Akriti?'

'Here I beg to differ; a wife's adultery is something tough to handle, but saying that vengeance against Akriti is the only thing that is putting you on this path to court women sounds sadistic, and if you say you only want to check how desirable you can still be to them, it sounds out-and-out narcissistic. But sure, if on the way you discover a few hidden truths, I am all for it.'

'God, this is all so convoluted,' Shiva heaves a long sigh.

'Yes it is, and I believe you know it; unfortunately, the trigger to set one racing towards the finishing line of truth is only pain. But the yearning somehow powers it along, right?'

'Yes, brother, I know; the journey appears exciting and tough at once.'

'Yes, and I am sure your logic will make it less tough for you. The man who can establish how Gandhi is greater than Krishna can easily wean women off their marriages,' Deven's always-smiling eyes smile some more.

Shiva too breaks into an unequivocal smile, revelling in the same old resonance of an abiding give-and-take friendship.

They joyously recall the debating competition in

college on the eve of Gandhi Jayanti, which aimed at bringing out a unique perspective on Gandhi; Shiva got the first prize.

'What a display of ingenuity it was!' Deven chuckles.

'But don't you agree with what I said?'

'Agree or disagree, I don't know, but it was cerebral gymnastics; can't one enjoy the sheer beauty of logic free from the burden of truth?

Shiva had passionately argued, 'Gandhi was transcendental in his fight for freedom. He didn't use violence against the British rule, and instead resorted to Satyagraha, which was a forked olive branch. It was a double-edged sword; with one it protested for the cause of freedom, and with another it tried to transform the adversary.

Could Krishna not have brought about the transformation within the Kauravas and avoided violence, instead of fomenting the deadly Mahabharata, the goriest bloodbath that Earth has ever known? Being divine and benevolent, he could have very well done that. Secondly, while Gandhi convinced people to fight nonviolently with his humane ways, Krishna persuaded Arjuna, who at first baulked at slaying his own kin, with his own theory of karma and godly duty, to engage in battle to uphold dharma.

And mind you, Krishna defeated the then largest army of this country, and Gandhi the largest empire of the world, except that Krishna had his invincible *Sudarshana chakra*, and Gandhi was completely weaponless. So who seems greater? Wouldn't it be Gandhi?'

Shiva looks at Deven with a brilliant flush; the pleasures out of the deeds done with heart never fade out of mind.

'But now, I wonder, how did you compare man with God?' Deven asks in awesome wonder.

'Krishna, I regard as a godlike being with human attributes, using lies, deception and subterfuge to a good end; that way I am justified in comparing the two, otherwise establishing that Man is greater than God would be a bit hazardous,' says Shiva lightly.

'Painting a god in human colours suits man better, otherwise what is the point in providing man with such perfect models who will be impossible to emulate, and condemn man as sinner?' Deven theorises.

'Yes, very true. Recognising this folly and its dangerous repercussions, man perceived Vishnu's avatar as the practical Krishna, after the earlier idealist, Rama,' Shiva says with his old conviction.

'So that the likes of you don't feel any pricking of conscience in courting many women at once,' Deven erupts into full-throated laughter in complete disregard of the stares directed at them by the other diners in the cafe.

'Now let us come back into our world. Why haven't you married?' Shiva asks Deven.

'I had promised myself that I would raise a family only when I could provide them something worthwhile, and the uncertain path I had chosen needed a focused struggle.'

'That means you want to marry now?'

'Yes, of course; I believe one should marry out of the need, not to enact a ritual. Now I really seek a stable companion who can support me, and yes I also wish to experience the joys of fatherhood.' Shiva notices Deven's voice echoing in the restaurant; most of the guests are gone, and the sounds of the winding-up of the lunch session are amplifying the emptiness.

'Hmm… fatherly instincts,' Shiva smiles a shrewd smile. 'Am I to suppose, you want to indulge in nothing else?!'

Deven tries to hide a bashful smile.

'What about coming h-home t-tomorrow? Meet A-akriti and Ankur; you have not m-met Akriti after our w-wedding, as f-far as I c-can recall,' Shiva's speech is definitely beginning to grow indistinct.

Deven also stutters a promise to visit soon, holding Shiva's hand in a warm shake.

Both make an exit. At night in bed, Shiva thinks fondly of his meeting with Deven. Recalling his lively youth, reliving his friendship, and releasing his hidden anxieties have done wonders for his nerves.

# The Sliced Moon

Your heart can make you fly. Your heart can arrest your flight. The heartbreak Akriti brought him propelled him on the journey of discovering other women and their marriages, and now it is Sana who seems to be arresting Shiva's journey towards other married women; rapidly seeping into his heart, turning him lovesick, insisting that they meet only in places where they wouldn't be spotted by acquaintances. In her own home, she is at peace. It's difficult to be noticed in an impersonal multi-storey complex. She manipulates their times together adeptly. She has learnt well the art of juggling her marriage and her affair, without endangering either.

Sana enters Shiva's chamber. Prashant is already sitting there.

'Sir, there is a mail from the ministry. A delegation is coming from Azerbaijan. The visitors include a high official from the Ministry of Energy. The focus of the delegation is promotion of foreign investment in the oil sector in Baku. They want to meet us, too, in that context.

This mail is addressed to you and the project head of our joint venture partner, Ms Zeba,' Sana explains.

'Zeba' brings alive 'hijab' in Shiva's mind.

'That's great,' says Prashant, taking the printout from Sana and reading it curiously. He continues, 'Oh, they have informed us well in advance—their visit is almost two months away.'

'That's really great, it will help us a lot, and we can request them for faster clearances.' Shiva's eyes brighten up; he being the project head, it would be quite an accomplishment for him to finalise this venture for his company.

'Informing us so much in advance indicates their enthusiasm. The time I was there, I felt that it is a country in a hurry, like a hungry man pouncing upon food after prolonged starvation. The failure of communism in the USSR has put the Commonwealth of Independent States on the path of capitalistic liberalisation. Hence, you can rest assured, clearances will be pretty fast,' Prashant elaborates.

'Yes, state control has not worked anywhere except China,' Shiva says.

'But China is not really communist; I feel it is capitalistic communism there.'

'Well phrased, Prashant! They have modified their communism to meet their economic aspirations.'

'And what about us?'

'Socialistic capitalism.' Shiva apparently looks struck by an exciting thought, and adds, 'Don't you think that the world must be having all possible combinations of capitalism and communism, but the hunt for the right order is still on?'

Sana senses that Shiva is getting into his intellectual mode. Prashant smiles with a prompt, 'Well said, sir.'

'It would be interesting to experience the switch-over,' Shiva says.

'You will have the experience; very shortly you have to visit there,' Prashant says.

The rest of the day is consumed by work and Sana.

The day over, Shiva reaches home. Shiva and Akriti have fallen into the rhythm of distant living under the same roof. Shiva has come to carefully ignore all of Akriti's talk and movements, while Akriti has got used to the indifference of Shiva to the affairs of home and his talking minimally to her, avoiding even the ritual tea-togetherness in the evening. On the contrary, she is feeling a sense of relief as Shiva's disinterest in the matters of home means his not losing his temper, which offsets the prickle his indifference causes her.

'You could at least talk to me in full sentences,' Akriti says, reacting to a curt 'OK' from Shiva to her query regarding how his day went.

'Why? What's wrong?'

'I've been seeing how you have turned silent on me;

from where does all the sweet talk stream out so often at night when you talk on the phone? God knows whom you talk to.'

'Think whatever you want to; I'm not bothered.' Shiva scuttles out with a deliberate indifference, but a strange pleasure soothes his heart, because he's been successful at making Akriti doubtful.

'I know you are seeing someone; you do whatever you want to do but at least treat me with the dignity I deserve.' Akriti sounds on the verge of tears.

'Isn't it what you are doing too?' Shiva asks, turning away from her.

'What? Are you suspecting *me*?' Akriti's meek words lack conviction.

'You know what you are doing and I know what I'm doing. So let's each mind our own business. You didn't like my concern with most of the matters at home as it is, so I am keeping aloof from them—and happier too.' The vengeance he is taking stops him from revealing his pain.

'But, you shouldn't be rude because that poisons the air.' Akriti as usual is bothered about the bitterness in the air, not in the heart.

'I appear how I am and sound how I feel,' says Shiva curtly and walks out of the sitting room with his cup of tea.

Shiva stops for a while in front of the study room to finish his tea and talk to Ankur about his studies before walking into his room to lie in his bed. The thought that Akriti has been affected by his indifference continues to give him a faint thrill.

'*Should I try to bring things back to normal?*' is a question his mind tosses around a bit, but no sooner than it appears, the memory of her telling him to carry on with his ways hurts his vanity, cementing his belief that she is buying her freedom by ignoring his affair. The shawarma man's statement, that after a certain stage, a wife needs only money and security from her husband, crosses his mind yet again, filling him with disgust. The thought of his wife being with someone else puts an end to any plans to reconcile; the institution of marriage doesn't melt away even under the fieriest sun of reason.

Fortunately, Sana has provided him with a much-needed anchor after an agonising turbulence.

Official matters have begun hotting up for Shiva with the deadline for the finalisation of the DPR and the project schedule nearing fast. A final meeting between the two main companies in the JV, the other major shareholders, and the consultants has been fixed up to complete the task of firming up their proposal which has to be submitted to the Ministry of Energy, Azerbaijan. They wish to have the final thing before the delegation from Azerbaijan arrives.

'I think the DPR is OK,' Zeba nods, looking at the projector.

'That's great,' Shiva smiles at Zeba. Every time Shiva looks at her, his gaze tends to stay a bit longer at the hijab she wears, the term 'sliced moon' crossing his mind. He reflects, '*Her skin has a golden sheen, her eyes are big and expressive, lined with* surma, *her mouth naturally pink, shapely but pouted a bit, which the lip gloss further magnifies into a noticeable succulence, her features are sharp—overall, she has a pretty face,*' he sums her up. *How beautiful would the "full moon" look!*'

'But yes, we need to modify the bankability report within a week,' Zeba says, her voice trained to convey corporate élan, the slight huskiness adding an attractive texture to it.

'Why not, the modifications are pretty minor... ' Shiva exhibits all the enthusiasm at his command. Talking with that black hole still in his mind, he finds the endeavour all the more strenuous; it is like trying to sleep with the constant buzz of a cricket piercing the night.

'...hope we can finish within a week,' Zeba completes Shiva's sentence for him loudly. He finds her flamboyance appealing. Zeba looks like a woman in control of her life—confident and zealous. She is of medium stature, and well-endowed without looking stocky, with her buttocks a bit heavier than her frame. There is both softness and firmness in her body, which makes her desirable.

So the project proceeds well on course.

'Sir, did you notice, that Azerbaijani officer was being very chummy with Ms Zeba?' Prashant says to Shiva after the meeting with the visiting delegation.

'It seems they already know each other.'

'I heard her company has already handled a project in Azerbaijan; moreover, the owner of the company is also a Muslim, having some connection there. That way it can help our project,' Prashant says to Shiva while they get into Shiva's car and head back to their office.

'That is good, but anyway our proposal is sound,' Shiva has always believed in letting his work do the talking.

'But what is this Agra thing, sir?'

'The Taj Mahal, of course. It remains the foremost attraction for foreign visitors.'

'Are you willing to accompany the delegation?'

'Not exactly, I am a bit confused over that decision,' Shiva says.

'But I feel you must go; the healthy intermingling between the government officials and the corporate sector definitely helps the cause of enterprise,' Prashant says.

'I agree, but "crony capitalism" comes in the way.'

Chatting about the project, they reach their office and separate to go to their respective rooms.

'Hi, how was the meeting?' Sana enters Shiva's chamber.

'It was pretty OK, how about you? Anything left to do today?' Shiva gives her a hug before moving on to his chair.

'Nothing urgent...' Sana sits in the chair across the desk.

'Please check the mails once more before leaving. I have go to Agra tomorrow,' Shiva says, and then explains the reason for his Agra visit.

'Oh that means passing the whole day without seeing you!' Sana's words induce in Shiva an exciting feeling of being desired passionately by a woman, something he had been badly missing.

'Oh darling, we'll make up for it later.' Shiva rises from his chair, reaches Sana, checks if the door is locked, even though a knock at his door before entering his chamber is mandatory for everyone, and plants a quick kiss on her lips.

Next morning Shiva leaves for Agra. His car follows the one transporting the government delegates; it is a company car meant for outdoor official visits. He can see Zeba accompanying the Oil Ministry's official in his car. Shiva chats with Sana for a while over the phone before nodding off. The music playing in the car is deepening the languor that getting up earlier than usual in the morning induces.

'Oh what a beauty it is! It is not for nothing that it is one of the wonders of the world.' The Azerbaijani official looks spellbound the moment he sees it.

'Sir, it is one of the treasures of India,' Zeba looks happy, watching the officer flush with admiration.

'You should say, "treasure of the world",' the official says generously.

Shiva is a little behind the two while they walk along, not very keen to get involved in their tête-à-tête on the Taj Mahal. They reach the main structure and position themselves in front of the intricate marble carvings. Zeba explains how long the mausoleum of Mumtaz Mahal had taken to be built, and how passionately Shah Jahan had been involved in its construction right through. Now they move to the inner sanctum where the king and queen lie in their tombs. While the officer and Zeba are engaged in animated chatter, Shiva remains wrapped in an unconscious indifference. He feigns sharing their feelings with forced smiles and nods, at best entering their conversations with token terms like 'really beautiful', 'architectural marvel' and so on.

'Hats off to the emperor! He gave the world probably the finest monument of love; see how he lies close by his beloved queen even in death,' the awe in the officer softens into tenderness.

'It is truly amazing that a king could love only one woman so passionately! His love for Mumtaz is truly matchless.' Zeba's face grows grave. 'How can a man love only one woman so intensely?'

Her emphasis on the phrase 'only one woman' instantly alerts the half-hearted attention of Shiva; he feels drawn in a bit.

'I feel this sublime white symbolises the absolute purity of his love for his queen, spotless like this white marble,' the officer is running out of words of praise.

Shiva itches to say something but resists, thinking, 'Expressing any contrarian opinion on such an occasion would be hardly polite!'

'Yes sir, truly untainted,' Zeba goes on.

'Let us look around a bit. The gardens and so many other places are worth a look here,' Shiva says, going down the stairs of the Taj Mahal.

'Yes, of course,' said the official. 'I have been so keen on seeing everything to do with it. Heaven knows when I can visit here again.'

Shiva leads them to the eastern side of the Taj. They walk through the garden and beyond to finally reach a tomb. Shiva stops there, and so do they.

'It is believed that Shah Jahan's first wife, Kandhari, was buried here,' Shiva invites the attention of the two.

'Was she also a queen of Shah Jahan?' the official asks.

'Not as far as I know; she is supposed to be his first wife, but she could never be the queen.' There is irony in Shiva's tone.

'Oh! I didn't see it when I visited here last,' Zeba says.

'Who will bother to visit this decrepit structure after

seeing the sublime Taj?' The sarcasm in Shiva's words grows amplified.

'But they could have maintained this one, too,' the official says, the euphoria leaving his voice.

'Sir, Kandhari in this decrepit tomb and Mumtaz in the sublime Taj; don't you feel this suggests Kandhari's relegation to a lonely place in life as well as death?' Shiva's meaning becomes more and more obvious.

Hearing Shiva, Zeba's face assumes a look of sadness, which invites Shiva's curiosity. The sliced moon, anyway, turns him curious whenever he meets her. He tries to decipher her face for her thoughts.

'Yes, well said,' the officer says, beginning to walk away, seemingly not keen on letting the discussion continue.

'If you permit I will complete what I was about to say,' Shiva looks at the Azerbaijani official.

'By all means,' says the man with a polite nod.

'You just said that the love of the King for Mumtaz was untainted, but don't you feel that his love was tainted with the humiliation of Kandhari? More for Mumtaz meant less for Kandhari,' Shiva says in a flurry, eager to get the words out. His companions are already walking away. Finding Zeba looking back at him, Shiva says, 'The pristine whiteness of the Taj also wears the gloss of Kandhari's tears.'

The three rejoin the rest of the delegates after stopping at some other monuments in the vicinity of the Taj. Then, they move to the hotel where lunch awaits them. Zeba still looks lost in her own thoughts, smiling only out of politeness and preferring to speak in monosyllables. The afternoon has been earmarked for the Agra Fort. They are supposed to reach Delhi early for the formal dinner.

On the way back to Delhi, Shiva engages again with Sana on the mobile; theirs is, after all, a new passion, yet to play itself out. As dusk approaches, he tries to grab a nap, conserving his energies for making conversation at the night's dinner. But as soon as he closes his eyes, he encounters the black hole again. Something that even thoughts of Sana cannot fill.

'Ms Zeba, I have great hopes for our project,' smiles Shiva over a glass of wine. 'It's all going so smoothly—not a problem in sight.'

They are at the formal dinner, sitting around tables which have been separately arranged for the evening. They have settled down to light chatter after exchanging the required courtesies with the government dignitaries of both the nations. The Azerbaijani official who had kept Zeba company throughout the day is sitting with his own countrymen. A live band is playing some soft music.

'You can call me just Zeba,' she says, sipping her fruit punch.

'Sure, Zeba!' Shiva looks at her, assessing her reaction to his sudden dropping of all formalities of speech.

'As for the project, yes, it should be just a matter of time before we bring about its complete success. By the way, have we stopped talking about anything else?' Zeba is one of those who don't believe in carrying shoptalk beyond office hours.

'Don't you drink?' Shiva asks, looking at her glass.

'It is prohibited for us,' she says, turning serious.

'Oh, you seem like a staunch follower of your faith,' Shiva says, his eyes fastened on her hijab.

Zeba is quiet for a while. Her lack of interest in Shiva's delving deeper into the subject is visible.

'What a beautiful collection of fish! Don't you just love those exotic colours,' Zeba says, her eyes sparkling at the large aquarium affixed to one of the walls in the restaurant.

'So you enjoy looking at aquaria?'

'Don't you like them? To me, they're like miniature oceans. I have one at home, though not, of course, as large,' Zeba enthuses.

'Its aesthetic appeal is undeniable… but….' Shiva places a cube of imported cheese in his mouth.

'But what?' Zeba says, biting into a vol-au-vent.

'Actually, I was reminded of something.' Shiva sips his wine faster, now.

'If it's not too personal, you can share it with me.'

'Nothing personal. A very close friend of mine wrote a poem on an aquarium; I loved it, and also translated it into English when we were in college.' It was Deven's poem.

'I would love to hear it.'

Shiva doesn't always open up this easily to relative strangers, but he finds himself reciting:

'This beautiful house of
glass with a
floating mosaic of tiny lives
Over the
pebbles, shells and corals;
the entire sea
squeezed into it;
the size of my heart.'

Coming to the end of the poem, Shiva wonders if Zeba has caught the gist of it.

'I understood it partly,' Zeba says, as if in reply to his unspoken question, 'but could you elaborate on the bit that says, "the size of my heart"?'

'Yes, why not? It conveys that the poet has mixed feelings on looking into an aquarium. He is actually apologetic about marvelling at the beauty of something that represents the captivity of the fishes.'

'Really a very touching depiction!'

'And now let me express the emotions which this poem aroused in me.' Shiva is now a bit tipsy, feeling the need to exercise his brain. 'This aquarium stands for the boundaries of tradition which are framed by man without logically examining them, and these fishes symbolise individuals who are left to live their lives within those defined boundaries.'

Zeba wordlessly puts down her mocktail. Shiva knows she has experienced the sentiments of the poem, and is pleased by her quiet gratification. '*But which part of her life does the verse touch upon*?' He longs to know. '*At the Taj, too, she seemed to be quite affected, as if reflecting on something tragic in her life.*' His curiosity flares, lending an urgency to his discovery of that part.

'Don't you feel these boundaries are more restrictive to women?' he encourages her to open up.

Zeba remains silent, her eyes downcast, but forces a faint smile on her face. Shiva realises she agrees with him.

Before Zeba could bring herself to speak, the friendly official walks up to their table, bringing his glass of scotch with him, with evident intention of joining them.

'Hope you are enjoying the evening,' he says, beaming widely. Shiva has stood up out of courtesy.

'Certainly, sir. How about you?'

'A very nice evening, and let me thank you, too, for a great day!'

'Happy that you enjoyed Agra,' Zeba says, returning fast to party behaviour.

'The Taj is simply fabulous, far more lovely than I

had even heard,' he enthuses, looking into Zeba's eyes. He turns his gaze to Shiva and says, 'I have to acknowledge it, you are very sensitive in your perceptions. I was touched by your unusual take on the two mahals.' High on whiskey, he struggles to stop nattering on. He finds himself speaking as a liberal not clinging blindly to the tenets of his religion but as a clear-sighted individual. Shiva smiles smugly while Zeba nods along, stealing an admiring glance at Shiva.

The three talk more before proceeding for dinner. The question Shiva had put to Zeba, about whether she agreed that tradition was harder on women, has not been replied to, because the official had interrupted their conversation. '*But would Zeba have answered*?' is the real question that persists in Shiva's head. '*Should I try getting closer to her*? *Somehow, I'm sure there is much within her to be discovered. Our relationship is purely professional, but will she entertain thoughts of something more intimate*?'

Shiva has consciously allowed himself to get sloshed tonight, which he does sometimes. He reaches home and, negotiating the scorn of Akriti over his apparently beyond-the-quota drinking, flings himself into bed. Zeba's secret sorrow keeps intriguing him, until the whiskey lulls him to sleep.

As Shiva gets busier with the new project, the black hole in his mind fades slightly. The next milestone to be reached is their visit to Azerbaijan with the final proposal.

The company has clubbed this trip with a visit to Italy by Shiva and his technical assistant, Rohit, to study the Tempa Rossa project. Formalities seeking the due permissions from Italy have already been processed. The Italian leg of the trip is to come about in three months.

'He is going to Jaipur tomorrow, so, we can meet,' Sana whispers to Shiva. Both have been desperate for each other, but resisted too many trysts; Sana because she wants to play safe and keep both sex and marriage going, and Shiva, because he still believes the shawarma man's adage: 'A bit less of everything makes life complete.' *If desire is a reality, so is the security and identity provided by marriage. Mother, father, husband, wife, son, daughter—all these constructs are indispensible to society.*

'Wonderful! At last!' Shiva erupts into excitement.

'Shall I say something? We are getting to meet after a long time; can we spend the whole day together? God knows when we will get to meet next,' Sana looks expectantly at Shiva.

'It's like you've read my mind!' Shiva is beside himself with joy. He can nearly smell her lust.

The following evening they meet; within minutes both of them feel the aftermaths of a blitzkrieg upon them. They exorcise the beast which has clamped them in its jaws all these days, and feed upon each other instead, hungrily. Then, passions stilled, they still don't realise how the evening passes. Time dilation, Shiva reminds himself.

While Sana's adventure continues, Akriti's path has taken a slight bend. Shiva's continued indifference and increasing distance have begun to play on her mind, which is evident from the diminishing frequency of her outings and the briefer exchanges on her mobile. She clearly suspects in Shiva's withdrawal, the lull before the storm. Shiva notices that she has noticed, deriving a momentary joy from spiting her, but not without the dull ache of knowing he and Akriti have fallen apart; the black hole stays put. But now, he has sailed far beyond her to seek other shores; once consigned to the wild currents of the ocean, it is nearly impossible to come back to the same shore.

☒

# Zeba Rises Like the Full Moon

Our most intense thoughts often prove to be the dictates of destiny. And since it so rules our lives, no matter how determinedly we try to terminate the journey breeding such thoughts, destiny fails us.

Shiva is packing his bags for travel to Azerbaijan, then Italy. He wishes Akriti and Ankur could join him in Italy as he has not been able to take them on a holiday for quite some time, but Ankur's exams have come in the way. He will plan a summer vacation with his family on his return to India. Few routines survive even the roughest tumults in life, the family holiday is one such.

Shiva and his technical assistant, Rohit, along with Zeba and her business partner, are ready to fly to Baku, the capital city of Azerbaijan. Shiva and Rohit will fly further on to Rome to study the Tempa Rossa project, while Zeba will fly back to India with her colleague.

'I had never expected this city to be so beautiful!' Shiva says to Zeba on the way to their hotel from Baku airport.

'Isn't it? I was really impressed when I came here last, almost two years ago,' Zeba says, looking out of the car window.

'What had brought you here?'

'I had come in connection with a project my company was trying to set up here, but somehow couldn't follow through.'

Shiva doesn't feel inclined to ask 'why'.

'Particularly impressive is the harmony in the colour of the houses along the way. All of them are fronted by white stone.'

'Yes, their government is very ambitious about their capital city. They are using the riches earned out of oil for its beautification. They plan to take it the Paris way.' Zeba sounds proud of her knowledge of Baku.

'Yes!' Shiva responds. 'The landscaping of the unused space by the sides of the roads is so well thought-out; the lush green grass and the brightness of the flowers! And that, too, in a region where the climate is not favourable to vegetation! They are the blossoms of a determined will,' Shiva concludes, sounding deeply impressed.

'They know perfectly well how much space to cover with construction and how much to spare for landscaping,' Zeba tells him. Shiva turns to watch the joy spreading over Zeba's face while she continues, 'Why can't we do this in India?

Shiva is uncomfortably reminded of the concrete jungle of Gurgaon. Shiva and Zeba are more comfortable with each other now, and speak together more easily.

'We can only think of giving our cities and countryside a face-lift,' Shiva says with a mix of sarcasm and distaste, 'only when the mammoth task of hauling our people elsewhere spares us.' The traffic jams in his city surface up in his mind.

'Very well said; you have a penchant for philosophy,' Zeba smiles, recalling the day in Agra which had concluded with such a sombre dinner.

'It's not philosophy but fact.'

'But not always can one show the other side of everything. Plus, I like the subtlety in your expression; you guided us to the Kandhari tomb to underscore your feelings about the Taj Mahal, rather than blurting them out at the Taj itself.' Zeba's admiration is shyly expressed.

'Thanks for the praise, but not everyone likes philosophy. Many find it to be a mental luxury,' Shiva says self-deprecatingly.

'I can't say about others, but I like talking to you because you always have something different to offer on a common subject.'

'That's pretty flattering to learn,' Shiva's eyes take on a twinkle.

The four of them arrive in two cars at the hotel, and check into their individual rooms. Zeba's and Shiva's rooms open on to the same corridor.

'I want to explore the place and its culture. Since you already know the city, you're the ideal person to guide me around it,' says Shiva.

'Do you want to go exploring today?'

'Not necessarily, we've got two full days ahead.'

'Any specific plans for today, then?' Zeba asks Shiva.

'Nothing specific. But a post-lunch siesta is a must to make up for the lack of sleep on the plane. And yes, I'd like to go for a swim in the evening. What about you?'

'I'd love to try out more local cuisines, and this city has got some very good restaurants. Are you interested in dining out?' Zeba feels burdened with the thought of spending her time alone.

'Sure, by all means. I, too, love good food—and drink, of course.' Shiva's eyes gleam with anticipation.

'Is 8 in the evening OK by you?'

'Oh, yes, absolutely fine.'

They go to their respective rooms. As soon as the hotel boy makes an exit, Shiva loosens his tie and lies down on the luxurious bed. His interest in Zeba has spiked—he is already sensing the dinner as an opportunity to discover the mysteries within her. A new place turns even strangers into friends.

A refreshing siesta followed by an invigorating swim has gotten Shiva into the spirit of adventure. He changes into a body-hugging black tee; frequent gymming has returned to him the luxury of sporting his favourite wear. His body looks really good now. His gymming has lent a machismo appeal to his tall and broad frame. '*I am looking genuinely handsome*,' he tells himself in the mirror.

Shiva calls Zeba when he's dressed, as they'd agreed, and she asks him to pick her up from her room. Moments later, she opens the door to the ring of the bell.

'Hope you had a good rest,' Shiva says, his voice thickening a little at the sight of the 'sliced moon'.

'Yeah, I had a long nap, and a shower,' Zeba says, sounding refreshed. Her gaze sweeps over Shiva appreciatively.

They go downstairs and get into the car that is at their service. Rohit and Zeba's subordinate have their own plans; water seeks its own level. Shiva and Zeba are driven to 'City Boulevard', the shopping and dining hub of Baku.

'It is a thriving place, and the festive ambience speaks of people growing rich fast,' Shiva says, deeply impressed. They have reached the City Boulevard.

'Yes, oil is pumping money into the economy. Released from the ideology of state control, it's booming,' Zeba sounds like a corporate woman.

'Well said, you! The extent of control should be governed by the ideology of the happiness of the people.'

They choose one of the best-known restaurants in Baku. 'Please decide what you think is best for the both of us on the menu,' Shiva says as they sit down at their table. 'You're the seasoned traveller!'

'For starters, we could go with skewers. They seem to have a good variety,' Zeba sounds excited.

'Sure. I'll order my wine. What about you?'

'I'll have something soft.'

'Have you never taken hard drinks?'

'Earlier, before marriage, on a few occasions when I took my sister out. We're very good friends. We used to indulge ourselves off and on.'

'So why did you stop it completely?'

'I never took it after marriage. I will have soft drinks,' Zeba repeats with an air of finality, cutting him short again, reminding him of the dinner in Delhi when he had asked a question in the same vein.

They place their orders for starters and drinks.

'What shall we have for the main course?' Shiva asks, trying to soothe the ruffled feelings his question about her drinking may have caused.

Zeba tells him about the famous dishes of Azerbaijan. They decide to order the classic kufta bozbash and mutton pilaf. 'Kufta bozbash is the national soup of the country,' she briefs him, 'and is made from meatballs, potatoes and peas boiled to a broth with saffron and turmeric. The pilaf, a mix of rice and meat, is flavoured with herbs peculiar to the region.' Zeba begins to grow animated again, pointing out the contrasting textures and colours of the dishes.

'The subject of food is so dear to a woman's heart!' Shiva laughs, enjoying her excitement. 'So I needn't worry about the right choice of food when you are with me,' continues Shiva, digging in. 'Now tell me which places are interesting to see here. I love to learn about places new to me.'

'You will love the palace of the Shirvanshahs, and also the Museum of Modern Art, and National Art Museum.'

'We could visit those tomorrow afternoon. The meeting with the oil officials is likely to be over by lunch.'

'Yes, let's. I will shop for some handicrafts too,' she says, bending delicately to chew at the chicken pieces on her skewer. Shiva can sense she is gradually mellowing.

'Don't you feel uncomfortable keeping your head always covered?' Shiva ends up asking her, encouraged by their burgeoning bonhomie.

'I am pretty used to it,' she says, curt again, the ice threatening to return.

'But can I say something? Just please don't take it personally. It is just my curiosity, not any advice I'm giving you.' Shiva searches her face for approval.

'It's OK, please go ahead,' she mellows down just as quickly.

'The little I have known of you so far tells me that you are a woman with a keen aesthetic sense—loving the colours of the fish in the aquarium, getting attracted to the colours even of food, knowing how much of the beauty spots of the city should to be covered, and so on and so forth. I mean to say, you have a discerning eye. I find such a woman keeping her head covered hard to rationalise. Is it by choice or…' Shiva stops himself from going further. He looks at Zeba with apprehension, trying to guess at what her response would be.

'I don't question inheritance,' Zeba regresses into seriousness, which, this time, is underlined with somberness.

'Fine. But let me clarify again that I didn't intend to question your wearing of a hijab, just wished to know your comfort level with it. Sorry if you…'

'It's OK.'

Shiva feels a bit guilty and tries to cheer her up by saying, 'Oh, and by the way, even a part of the whole looks pretty.' Slice of the moon.

Shiva's words prompt Zeba into a shy acknowledging nod to his compliment.

Just then, their main course arrives. Shiva calls for another small bottle of wine, enjoying his tipsiness. Zeba can see that he is also loving the food, and some of her confidence returns. The main course over, it is the turn of dessert. They choose *Shekerbura* which is one of the most popular desserts in Azerbaijan. The sweet patty is stuffed with almonds, hazelnuts, and walnuts mixed with honey. Shiva loves its crunchy texture, and is pleased with Zeba's choice of food for him.

'You have ordered a fabulous dinner,' he says gratefully, although he is secretly disappointed by her reticence in other matters.

By the time they leave the restaurant, she is smiling happily again.

They reach the hotel and bid each other a friendly 'good night'. They have decided to meet early for breakfast in the café of the hotel to discuss the nitty-gritties of their proposed meeting with the officials of the Ministry of Energy. Both of them feel upbeat about their project.

Retiring to bed, Shiva calls home to talk to Akriti and Ankur. He is missing his son, recalling the game of chess they played a day before he left, and Ankur's animated narration of a Harry Potter movie he had seen. Then, Shiva settles down to reading Sana's amorous messages; she has been in touch with him nearly every step of the way. He sends her a message and almost immediately receives a reply asking him why he hasn't texted her for a while. He calls her and they keep chatting till Sana is compelled to sign off because she has heard her husband returning.

'I am happy with the meeting,' Zeba says, coming out of the ministerial offices the next day.

'I am really impressed with the way they have simplified the procedure,' Shiva comments.

'Sir, I feel we are well on course,' Rohit catches up with Shiva, showing his involvement, while Zeba walks alongside.

'Yes, you have all worked hard, now let's pray it goes through,' Shiva bucks up his subordinates like a good boss.

'Let's all have lunch together,' Zeba complements Shiva's congratulatory spirit.

'Sure,' Shiva says.

Shiva and Zeba enter their car while the other two get into theirs. They go to a nearby restaurant and share a table. Over lunch they plan their sightseeing. While Shiva is interested in visiting the palace and the museum, the other two are keen on seeing the Burning Mountain, a natural gas fire which stays aflame in an area outside Baku, and roaming in the City Boulevard.

'I had passionately wanted to see his paintings,' Shiva says to Zeba, sounding ecstatic. They are walking past the works of Azim Azimzade, one of the most renowned painters of Azerbaijan. They are in the National Art Museum after seeing the Palace.

'What do you find extra special about him?' Zeba asks.

'I like his boldness in questioning the social and political traditions with reason. He celebrates humanism, his art stimulates the mind into free-thinking.' Shiva is lingering before the watercolour *The Girl Was Born*, one of Azimzade's best. He continues, 'You can make out how touchingly he depicts the issue of gender discrimination. See how the husband has turned away from his wife, expressing his indignation at the birth of a girl child?'

'Yes, true,' Zeba feels drawn in by his remarks, and looks thoughtful.

They continue past some more of Azimzade's works, absorbed in the emotions his creations arouse.

'This one,' says Shiva excitedly, 'this is the point I was trying to make at the Taj in Agra when we looked at the tomb of Kandhari'. Shiva has a feeling of déjà vu. He calls Zeba's attention to *Old Wife and A New One*. The painting shows how the new wife of a Muslim man is sitting beside him comfortably on the central seat, expanded with swagger, relishing the delicacies laid before them, while the old wife with her young child sits neglected in the corner. Zeba's face grows eclipsed by sadness. Shiva resumes, 'Does this painting not evoke instant compassion in the beholder? How can this man making merry with his new wife be so insensitive to his first wife's feelings of neglect and humiliation? She, who was the mistress of the house not so long ago? Isn't it cruel?'

While Shiva is immersed in his own delivery on seeing the painting, Zeba has moved ahead, seemingly uninterested in seeing anything more. Shiva notices her absence after a short while, and thinks, '*It is her response to the poorer mahal in Agra amplified*.' He remorsefully watches her walking away, regretting having in some way depressed her or caused her to remember some sadness in her past. He catches up with her, and they walk out, neither of them saying a word.

Once out in the sunshine, he makes another attempt to cheer her up. 'Shall we have some ice cream?' he asks her sympathetically.

'Yes, we could,' Zeba says, knowing that remaining silent would add to the unease. She tries to shrug her sadness off.

Both make an exhibition of enjoying their ice cream, describing its flavour and texture to make up for each other's discomfiture. Finally, the flavour of the ice cream changes the flavour of the air. It is a change from art to matter, from the sublime to the mundane.

'Now let's us go to City Boulevard and unwind,' Shiva says. He has taken it upon himself to bring her completely back into friendly elements.

'Sorry, Shiva, but I am feeling too tired for that. I'd like to go back to the hotel and rest a bit.'

'Sure, in that case I'll come along. I feel like a swim.'

'But why would you sacrifice your evening?'

'I'm not sacrificing anything. I mentioned the Boulevard because I thought shopping never failed to pep up a woman.'

'Oh, so nice of you!' Zeba is touched. On the way to their hotel, they chat like friends.

'So where do we have our dinner?' Shiva asks, while Zeba unlocks her room.

'I think I will have it in my room.'

'We could have it together in the hotel restaurant,' Shiva proposes. He can sense she is still unhappy within.

'I feel like staying back.'

Shiva says a reluctant 'As you wish' and takes her leave.

Zeba goes to her room after exchanging a deflated 'bye', throws her bag on the couch, sheds her hijab, and lies flat on the bed. She lies with her eyes wide open, blankly looking up at the ceiling.

Shiva changes immediately and goes for a swim in the ice-blue pool. He decides to order room service for dinner as he is suddenly tired himself. He is curious to read the English translation of the Quran which is kept at the side of the bed, but gets into a chat instead with Sana. Neither Shiva nor Sana are yet sated with each other. But after his talk with Sana, Shiva nervously calls Zeba's room to inquire about her well-being.

'Have you taken your dinner?' Shiva asks.

'Not yet, shall order it now. What about you?'

'I will have it in a short while.'

'OK...' Zeba pauses.

'So when do we leave for our visit to the oil field tomorrow?' Shiva prolongs the talk.

'We can leave at a comfortable time. There is not much left to do tomorrow. We can even have a late breakfast.'

'Is 9:30 fine?' Shiva asks.

'Yeah, sure,' Zeba pauses again. Then, not knowing what to talk about, she softly says, 'So... goodnight.'

'Goodnight,' says a chastened Shiva. He genuinely wants to be with her a little longer in the evening, but her response dampens him.

It is 10 at night. Shiva is lying in his bed after finishing his dinner. He begins reading the Quran, but feels a bit disoriented. He puts the book back on the stand, and switches on the TV to fill the void. Just a little later the doorbell to his room rings.

'Zeba, you? All well?' Shiva is perplexed, standing at the door.

'Yeah, all well, I couldn't sleep, so thought of chatting with you for a while—but only if you are not sleepy or busy otherwise,' Zeba smiles shyly, enjoying the amazement on Shiva's face.

'Yeah, by all means, please come in,' Shiva's eyes catch the change in Zeba's looks. She is dressed in a black churidar with a matching kameez. The dupatta around her head replaces the hijab, with the surplus length flared down upon her bosom like a scarf. The black attire looks very attractive against her golden skin, glowing as it does in the yellow light of the lamp.

He vacates the couch, removing his laptop to make room for her. She is blushing, '*What must he be thinking*!'

Shiva is trying to look like he's not thinking at all, except of her comfort. 'So, the day was good, the meeting was quite satisfying, you must be pleased,' he says, trying to put her at ease.

'Yes, definitely satisfied,' Zeba mumbles.

'Would you like a coffee?'

'Thanks, I'm fine.'

'So, how was the evening?' Shiva can sense a storm within her waiting to expend itself.

'Are you still curious to know why I walked out of the museum?' Zeba suddenly makes a sharp turn in their conversation, such as it is.

Shiva is taken aback, momentarily turned speechless. He is not able to decide how to respond in spite of his growing excitement in her mysterious presence. Aware of Shiva's discomfort, Zeba breaks the silence to say, 'I want to share with you something about myself. You are a man who views life from the point of view of an individual, and this humane perspective appeals to me. Plus, I find you genuinely interested in knowing me for myself. I know my responses have been erratic.'

The sight of a softening Zeba calms Shiva's frazzled nerves.

'Yes, sure, you are most welcome, it's my pleasure,' Shiva's words tumble over each other in their gladness.

'I can very well replace the "old wife" sitting neglected in the corner in the painting by Azimzade,' Zeba says, looking directly into Shiva's eyes.

Shiva is shocked into pausing for a reply. '*Am I really hearing right*?' he wonders.

'I'm sorry if I sounded thoughtless in the museum,' he manages to bring out finally. 'I happen to know that the incidence of polygamy in your religion is less prevalent amongst the educated class—and is falling.'

'Maybe less, but it has not vanished.' Before Shiva can respond, she says, 'My husband married a woman much younger than him. She was quite attractive as well. On her part, she was attracted to his wealth.'

'So, he is a rich man!'

'Initially it was I who supported him when he was trying to set up his business—we shared a good relationship, more or less, then. Later, the business clicked and he made some good money. One fine day, he decided to marry this woman who worked in his office.' Zeba is letting it all come out rapidly.

'Didn't you object?' Shiva's amazement overtakes his sympathy.

'How could I object? It is something permitted by our religion in our country.'

'Then, at least, come away? After all, you're a working woman.'

'It's very difficult for a woman to live alone.' Zeba is being practical and bitter at the same time. 'The beast in the husband is able to protect you from the many beasts howling at you all at once.' She thinks further and adds, 'And how could I deprive my son of his father?' Her voice turns teary, and she looks down.

'But the legal system of our country has also begun looking at polygamy unfavourably,' Shiva's astonishment at an educated woman like Zeba bearing all this refuses to diminish.

'Many a time, we have to prefer peace to justice,' Zeba smiles in sadness, tears challenging her shyness now.

'I am extremely sorry...' Shiva falls short of words.

'You know you have to accept the sanction of religion in the name of piety.'

'But do you believe that polygamy is blessed by God?'

'How does my belief matter as long as it is sanctioned? It has been an age-old practice,' Zeba dodges the question.

'I find that Islam is a great religion which talks of the happiness of man, and professes peace, compassion, and universal brotherhood, and my notion doesn't just spring from my gut. Whatever little I have read supports my notion,' Shiva is careful not to hurt Zeba's sentiments.

'Great. You have read about our religion also! So what do you have to say about polygamy?' Zeba's spirits sounds restored.

'You know, I was a fairly good debater in my college days. Once I had participated in a debating competition on the subject of polygamy. In one of the discussions it was brought out that polygamy was practised out of economic need. Have you heard of the Battle of Uhud?'

'Though I am not very keen on reading about religion, but I do know a bit about it. Still, I would love to know what you have to say.'

'The battle of Uhud took place between the early Muslims and the Quraish Meccans. There was a colossal loss of human life, a huge number of men died. It meant society was left with a vast number of widows and orphans. Hence, out of the compulsion to provide emotional and economic security to them, men were allowed to marry more than one woman, provided they would be able to fend for them all well enough. Thus, polygamy, as far as I know, emerged from compassion,' Shiva explains to Zeba.

Zeba looks at him with sombre admiration. 'What an irony it is! A practice which is rooted in compassion is now coming to violate the same value? Where did the compassion of that thoughtless man in Azimzade's watercolour vanish to, while he was putting his first wife through such utter neglect and humiliation?' Zeba begins to sob, but continues through her tears, 'I know how painful it is to be displaced as the mistress of the house. I know a man loses his desire for the same woman with the passage of time, but still, watching her man with another woman right under the same roof, facing the humiliation of the authority over the household getting snatched away…' tears finally hijack her voice.

'*Here it is not religion but we who are to be blamed; we have not allowed many traditional norms to evolve over time in accordance with the needs of man and society; alas, if truth and tradition could converge*!' Shiva thinks silently.

Shiva feels like going to her to console her, but hesitates. He knows that the proximity to a sad woman brings about its own kind of desire, and that feeling is already growing in him. '*Is Zeba another milestone on my journey?*'

Still, the sadness of Zeba propels Shiva on. He rises from his bed and steps towards Zeba who is now weeping helplessly. Shiva thinks, '*Is it the same Zeba, the no-nonsense, successful corporate woman? How quickly can the Himalayas, the mother of mountains, turn so suddenly into Tethys, the mother of seas?*' Her face is now buried in her palms. Ultimately, Shiva touches her shoulder. She covers his hand with her palm and looks up at him. Her eyes are awash in kohl-black tears. Zeba slowly removes the dupatta from her head. Shiva is suddenly reminded of Sana uncoiling her hair when they met first in her house. Dupatta shed, the sudden sight of his full moon, the full blossom of her face, takes his heart by storm. The woman in front of you can drive out all notions of fidelity. Here, 'Sana' in his mind gets eclipsed by 'Zeba' in the moment.

'I'm sorry I made you cry, I feel hugely guilty,' Shiva says, adding, 'May I say something?'

She conveys a silent 'yes'.

'Smothering such a beautiful blossom doesn't befit a woman of such artistic sensibilities.'

Zeba suddenly breaks away from him and runs out of his room, leaving him in a welter of confusion. '*Her marriage I know about, but what about her desire*?' He asks himself. '*Does she not feel pressed to seek it? Didn't the desire in her seek me just a while back? I thought she wanted me to console her, love her, make love to her...*' Shiva remains wrapped in these thoughts throughout the night.

The next day they meet at the breakfast table, and both try to act like nothing had happened the night before, feigning a deeper involvement in the project than they genuinely felt. Shiva is amazed by her dexterity in dispelling the mood of a few hours ago. Sitting in the car on their way to the oil field, Shiva is able to observe Zeba, intermittently becoming informal, then receding into professionalism. Sometimes, her hands brush his, and off and on she seems to lean into his shoulder. Shiva deciphers it to be deliberate rather than accidental. He feels stirred, with the image of last evening's full moon coming back in his mind. But then he thinks again, '*So far*

*I have never consciously tried to win her body; my interest in her was purely intellectual, just wishing to discover the reasons behind her mysterious responses to my talk about the trials and tribulations of women. As for her, I feel she is attracted to me. But the day is still not over, we have got tonight at our disposal…'*

'What's the plan for the evening?' he asks her innocently on the way back to the hotel. 'Are you going to treat me to few more kinds of cuisine?' They are through with their visit and their lunch.

'Yes, we can go out to eat in the evening. I thought of taking a quick look at the Burning Mountains this afternoon, but now I want to go back and rest a little.'

'You have the full afternoon to rest.'

'But I will have to sleep early; it is an early morning flight for me to Delhi,' Zeba says.

'For me as well; it's a long journey for me. I have to change my flight at Istanbul for Rome.'

They reach the hotel. Shiva takes a restful nap before setting out for a swim. In between, he chats with Sana for a good half-hour, and today their amorous exchanges are laden with sexual longing.

But Zeba is restless, struggling with something within her. She doesn't sleep well.

The two go for an early dinner, as planned. This evening, Zeba gets Shiva to try some more local dishes: the traditional yoghurt soup, pilaf, and bakhlava as dessert. Shiva enjoys them thoroughly. Both behave abnormally normal, as if nothing has happened between them. But both keep searching for signs of the last night on each other's faces. Zeba continues to momentarily slip into strange intimacies; she touches his hands twice unconsciously during dinner while sharing a laugh.

They are back at the hotel; it is 9:30 pm. Reaching the corridor to their rooms, both of them get caught up in a prolonged conversation. Tonight, bidding goodnight is taking a bit longer.

'So, it has been a nice trip,' Shiva says.

'It has been really good,' Zeba says happily. After talking for a while on generalities, they bid 'good night' to each other. Shiva suddenly feels sad with the thought of Zeba ultimately not turning into another milestone for him.

Shiva's mind takes another dive into the medley of marriage, desire and the varied orders created by man for serving his needs; the black hole gets magnified. It is almost 10:30 at night. Shiva feels uncomfortable, struggling to sleep.

The doorbell rings just as he dozes off. Shiva wakes up with a jerk, switches on the bed lamp at his side and gets up to open the door. He is gobsmacked by what confronts him. It is Zeba again at the door, miserable with blush. She enters his room. Shiva closes the door and follows her to the couch on which she has ensconced herself.

'All well?' Shiva knows that all is OK, but it is a question he has to ask. She is again clad in a churidar-kurta, tonight all red, with the dupatta tied over her head. The redness of her attire resonates with her ever-reddening blush, making her irresistible in his eyes.

'Yes, all well. Did I disturb you?' Zeba knows she hasn't really; it is just to lend a feminine garb to her bold passions. He catches her eyes on his chest, still in the tight tee he'd admired himself in earlier. She sheds her dupatta and leans languidly back, inviting his attention to her breasts, heavy with the promise of succulence. Shiva delights in seeing their clear contours for the first time, thinking breasts have not marred this woman. He bends over her, takes her silken cheeks between his palms and kisses her lips probingly. She fiercely takes his tee in her fists, pulling him down against her own yielding body. Their lips still locked, Shiva settles himself down upon his knees. She impatiently leans back and drags her kurta off, releasing the breasts from their cage, offering them to Shiva's craving hands. '*It is a roaring proclamation of freedom from captivity*,' exclaims his mind, turning him wilder. He too yanks his tee off, and the two get locked in a tight hug in a flash. Shiva is now feeling her throbbing breasts against his chest, marvelling at the sensation. His tongue flickers deeper into her mouth, conveying his desperation to discover all her secret, unseen places. She pushes him down flat on the floor, and stretches out to switch off the bed lamp nearest her. The lights filtering from the glass door fill the room with a throbbing translucence, promising Shiva a night of passion. His hands frenziedly travel over her fulsome folds of her body, his fat fetishism coming to the fore. She rides him lustily, making him reach deep within her so she can rejoice in all the sensations denied to her for so long, while Shiva rejoices along. They finally collapse against each other's bodies, spent with a joyful weariness. Even in the semi-darkness, Shiva can see her face shining through sweat and tears with a soulful flush.

Suddenly he feels another kind of wetness: the trickle of her tears on his neck. Filled with passion again, they traverse the journey within each other once more, this time in the warm bath of his equally tearful joy.

'While I can understand your tears, can I ask you something?'

She mumbles a feeble 'yes'.

'What made you choose me for letting out your vengeful suppressed desires?'

'Vengeful?'

'Let's not get into why I said that. I know the fury in the passion you exhibited is the handiwork of the revenge against what you have had to bear. Please tell me why you chose me for this catharsis?' Now Shiva tries to understand the Zeba chapter of his journey.

'I have already shared that. I found you to be a man

who is quick to spot the suffocation of an individual under a social order, a man who could see the darkness of the forlorn tomb of Kandhari even under the dazzle of the thriving Taj, and of course, you are the "one step forward and one step backward" kind of man, not in a desperate hurry at the sight of a woman. It intensely appealed to me. I feel surprised by my own reaction.' Zeba gradually gets up and dresses, trying to overcome her shyness at what transpired between them minutes ago. Once dressed and tidied up, the corporate lady in her is back.

She stays hardly for a few uncomfortable moments before walking out of Shiva's room saying briskly, 'I feel we won't be like this together again.' She won't take any such risk again in India, in the interest of the father of her son. Shiva calls to her retreating back, 'Zeba means beauty, and tonight I felt you lived up to your name.'

'*I will kill his seeds with the pill. Science has made possible my surrender to him complete, or did I just surrender to his mind? Alas, if I could be the mother of the offspring of such a beautiful mind!*' Zeba is gripped with these thoughts on her way back to her room.

Zeba gone, Shiva retreats into his much-celebrated mind, still lying on the floor. A memory of Sana rushes to instill guilt in him, but he meets it equably, thinking, '*It is the work of destiny. I was just curious to discover the mystery behind Zeba, I never tried to attain her. It is only since she visited my room last night that the wish to physically attain her made its way into me. I only spoke to her a few truths, and they plucked her from her marriage to drop her in my lap. How wonderful is the ecstasy of yet another victory! But why this guilt? Sana rankles in my heart. Deven was wrong when he said I would get to taste guilt-free desire on this journey after getting unhooked from Akriti.*' Withstanding the last vestige of guilt over Sana, he philosophises that while plucking a rose, the prick of its thorns is inevitable. The tryst with such thrill is always a bit thorny… And here he lets the matter rest.

☒

# The Fantasy Flight to Italy

The determination of a goal leads to action, and the fiery determination to attain that goal naturally brings strategy to the action.

After his tryst with Zeba, Shiva's resolve to continue the journey revives, having overcome the mellowing influence of Sana. Now, the excitement of understating the delicate balance between marriage and desire takes precedence over both his lust for revenge and the impulse to prove how attractive to the opposite sex he can still be.

Akriti, Sana and Zeba have already given him some knowledge of how both monogamy and polygamy fall deficient in serving the physical and emotional needs of man in totality, but to bring absoluteness to the truth, he proposes to himself, '*Let me test it as empirically as possible. While I appreciate Socrates' view that it is the mind which discovers the truth independent of experience, I don't completely discard the role of Aristotle's "experience" in the discovery of truth. Shouldn't I get to know some other women and their experience of marriage?'* Throughout his journey, often slipping into memories of his passionate encounters with Sana and Zeba, he keeps finding to his dismay the black hole.

Shiva lands in Rome, excited about this much-awaited visit to his dream destination. He has clubbed his itinerary for the Tempa Rossa visit with a weekend which he has planned to completely devote to the Vatican City, to see, for the first time, the fabulous Sistine Chapel. Already fantasising about the paintings and sculpture of Michelangelo, he checks into his hotel.

'Tomorrow morning, we have to get ready fast, and start out immediately after an early breakfast,' Shiva says to Rohit.

'It is quite a long drive as far as I know, so let's do just that,' Rohit concurs.

'Reaching early gives us adequate time to complete our work; the day after, too, we have to start back for Rome by noon.'

'I know you are pretty excited about visiting the Vatican, sir.'

The two set out for Basilicata the next day. During the drive, Shiva quickly gets in touch with Sana as he couldn't get connected to her the day before. '*She must be in the office by now...*' Shiva calculates the time-lag. After a talk with her, Shiva begins instructing Rohit on the work ahead of them. Basically, they are to study the finer aspects of the project, do some number-crunching, and wrap up in less than two days.

They complete the work to their satisfaction, and finally, it is Saturday morning and Shiva is left completely to himself. Having finished his breakfast early, he sets out, eager to make the most of his weekend in Rome. He explores the incredibly beautiful city at random, excited by everything, even the sweet sound of Italian being spoken around him, the wide-eyed tourists sharing his wonder at the monuments, until it's time to join the Vatican Museum guided tour he had booked on the first day he had arrived.

It was quite an endeavour—a huge rush, security check, and collecting audio headsets—before Shiva's group arrives in the courtyard of the museum. Here, the guide explains to them the layout of the Vatican City, telling them how this museum including the residence of the Pope forms an independent country. When the guide points to the exterior of the Sistine Chapel, Shiva's excitement surges uncontrollably.

'Let's go down into the lawns which exhibit the replicas of Michelangelo's famous paintings on the theme of the Book of Genesis on the ceiling of the Sistine Chapel. I shall explain them there because talking and photography inside the chapel is prohibited,' the guide briefs the group. Its members have already started moving down. Shiva notices he is the only Indian in the group of about 20 tourists.

'This is the famous one, *The Creation of Adam* by Michelangelo,' intones the guide. 'You are shown how God, floating in the heavens after creating man, releases him down upon Earth. You see the pain in the separation between God and man, see how their fingers don't meet after God has transmitted life into him, how the realm of God appears widespread, while that of man's Earth is limited, and the level of man is lower than that of God's—it suggests the superiority of God to man…'

Shiva is gripped by the enormity of the theme, his mind a melee of questions and perceptions. He feels stilled amidst the crowd; the rest of the group members are excitedly engaged in the guide's well-rehearsed flow of explanation, flooding him with queries about the types of colours, the styles used in the art, and their relative age. The guide is just a guide, Shiva thinks, he's no philosopher.

'If you were to hide the figure of Adam in the painting, then, who would imagine the unseen heaven, and who would be left to call the image above him God?' Shiva challenges him.

'But why would anyone want to hide Adam? I didn't get your question, sir.' The guide looks thoroughly out of his depth. One of the women in the group draws a bit closer to Shiva, looking at him curiously.

'You made Adam inferior, finding him at the lower level in the visual, and treating Earth limited vis-à-vis the widespread heaven,' retorted Shiva. 'I feel man and God are on an equal footing, as God needs Adam to call Him God, and heaven needs Earth to exist; to me it just depicts the descent of man from heaven to Earth.'

The guide looks askance; Shiva can understand his embarrassment. He is not here to take such queries.

'Sir, I have to tell all of you in my group many more things, and about many more paintings. So, let us not, per favore, stay for too long at any one fresco,' he says, nervously hurrying them on. Shiva stays fixed where he is, his interest in the guide fizzling out. But he notices that the woman beside him is still looking at him intently, apparently tempted to talk to him.

'Excuse me,' the woman approaches him with a gentle smile, reducing the volume of the audio.

'Yes...' Shiva says, smiling back while removing his earplugs.

'That was really a good question,' she comments.

'Thanks!'

The group is engaged with the guide, while the woman lingers in his company.

'Have you been here before?' the woman asks.

'No, this is my first visit,' says Shiva, still looking on enchanted at the painting.

'Have you noticed something interesting?' the woman asks hesitantly.

Shiva finds her a welcome recipient of his views. He says, 'I am contemplating the shape of the shell behind the image of God, the red drape around Him, that green scarf shown to be falling away…' Shiva is now looking at her.

'What is so special about them?' Before Shiva can reply she says apologetically, 'I hope I am not disturbing you. It's just that your question to the guide fascinated me. I feel it may be more interesting to listen to you.' By now they have shifted a little distance away from the group.

Shiva has some sense of the fact that Westerners don't hesitate in interacting freely with strangers on the topics which interest them; they don't allow shyness to come in the way of knowledge.

'Not at all,' he says putting out his hand. 'I'm Shiva.' Despite his fascination with the painting, Shiva has already noticed that the woman has a wonderful height, lovely figure, and a pretty face. Her firm breasts, as suggested by the cut of her blouse, catch his fancy. Typical Renaissance breasts, and a generous butt tightly encased in jeans, combine to hint at an alluring succulence. Who is the lucky guy to have such a beautiful wife?

'And I'm Mary,' says this vision, putting out her own exquisitely manicured little hand to clasp his.

'Is it your first visit, too, Mary?'

'No, I have been here many times before. Since I live in Florence, coming to Rome is not a big deal.'

The knowledge that she is Italian—in spite of her unaccented English—fills Shiva with thoughts of exciting possibilities of strengthening, and maybe heightening, their acquaintanceship. '*Beautiful, curvaceous too, and Italian! She appears to have stepped out of a Renaissance painting*,' he crows to himself.

'You wanted to ask me something?' Shiva is now eager to please. Shiva's gaze shifts to the replica again.

'Yeah, I wished to know what was so special about the painting.' Mary has turned unmindful of the guide.

'You know, *The Creation of Adam* remains one of the most discussed works of art; it has invited various interpretations, and I was trying to figure out one of them.'

'You sound like you already know much about these works. Anyway, what is that?' Mary asks, her eyes bright with interest. Shiva notices, in the fleeting moment he looks at her again, the shiny blue mascara on her lashes, to match the blue of her eyes that are slanted upwards.

'Doesn't that shell-like shape in the background of the figure of God anatomically resemble the human brain?' asks Shiva of Mary. 'If you look at it carefully, you can discern the cerebrum, the brain stem and the frontal lobe.' Shiva suddenly stops, wondering if Mary is aware of these anatomical details, and if he is bombarding Mary with boring biological jargon. 'Sorry, I never bothered to ask whether you are aware of the parts of the brain.'

'Not in detail, but I have seen the odd diagram, and I see now what you mean,' she says, her head turned to the replica. Flashing a glance at her, Shiva is struck with the symmetry of her long neckline and her tall frame.

'But what is the point you want to make?' she asks searchingly. 'You mentioned some interpretation you came across.'

'It has been interpreted as God transmitting intellect, which is the real divinity, to Adam through His finger. You can see Adam's finger stretched out there, receiving it from God; it is intelligence which makes man the supreme creation of God,' Shiva finds himself speaking with passion.

Mary says, looking enchanted, 'Amazing, such great works of art are so stimulating!'

'Quite true, and the perspectives they inspire can be as many as the number of people on this Earth. Anyone with intelligence can interpret things in his own unique way; that is what being man is about.' Shiva disengages his gaze from the painting, and smiles exclusively at Mary.

'Yes, anything amusing?'

'I feel tempted to tell you my own interpretation.'

'Of course, most welcome.'

'Can't I interpret it as Adam's brain conceiving God and conceptualising the belief that God created man?'

'You mean to say that man conceived God?'

'Precisely; not knowing where we have come from, we conceived an unseen entity, God, believing that He created us. This thought gives us a lot of solace; the artist may be wishing to convey this philosophy through this particular piece of art.'

'Quite likely, but unseen as God may be, He is so powerful that we turn to Him for so many answers in life, especially when we are sad and without hope,' Mary says, twisting the ringlets of her hair, which invites Shiva's attention to its golden colour.

'Very true. That is the magical power of belief.' Shiva waves his hand around, indicating the void, and continues, 'When it is nothing, your belief can call it anything, make it everything—don't you think that God is the answer to our questions because He himself is the question?'

'True, but man still craves to sense God.'

'Well said! That's why Adam's finger doesn't meet God's—he can't touch Him, but only sense Him.'

They suddenly overhear the guide talking about 'original sin' in the collage of the replicas. Mary starts, 'Oh, we are still talking about the same work; so many works yet to be… '

'Yeah, I know, but I'm not in a hurry. Since I have read a bit about a few of these famous works, I want to observe them keenly, and reflectively too.' Shiva sounds uninterested in the guide.

'But we need him to guide us into the museum, so we'll *have* to follow him,' Mary says, judging from her experience of earlier visits.

'Fine, but I believe he is going to spend quite some time there. The works of the Sistine Chapel captivate anyone, no matter how often they have seen them.'

'Same for me too. The Sistine Chapel is the prime attraction on a visit to Rome, and more so now when I can relish them better with you,' Mary says, revealing her intentions to continue in his company.

Meanwhile, the guide, spurred by the restlessness of a few in the group decides to prepone the break for photography and water. His group disperses for a while. It seems only natural that Shiva and Mary are together. Their interest in photography ends with a selfie and a solo click against the background of the museum. They sit in a trattoria in the lawns; Shiva settles for a soft drink, while Mary orders an ice cream. They continue talking eagerly, getting freer with each other. Shiva has told her about himself in some detail, spurred by her obvious curiosity to know more about him.

Now it's Mary's turn.

'Tell me something about your family.' Shiva says.

'My family means only me and my sister.'

Shiva pauses for a second before asking 'Marriage?' He guesses her age to be around thirty-five.

'This needs telling you about me in a bit more detail.' Mary smiles, enjoying the questioning look of Shiva.

'Sure.'

'I live in Florence with my sister,' she begins. 'Neither of us is married. We keep ourselves involved in various charitable works like orphanages and old-age homes. Money is not an issue as my father was a very rich man and he has bequeathed a fortune to us, two of us being his only children. Both of our parents are dead. It was our conscious decision not to marry as we saw our parents living a turbulent married life; they were incompatible in their views, quarrelled a lot and were unfaithful to each other. I never saw them happy together. We girls studied in a convent, and that is when, listening to the discourses on God and religion, we got deeply influenced. We perceive pain and death as being the result of disobedience to God, what they call the original sin. Initially, both of us thought of becoming nuns, but we found the regimen of obedience to be too tough to observe. I specially love my freedom. I want to move out and around seeing places. But we have resolved to not get into any temptation, and observe chastity. So we are getting to live life exactly the way we want.'

During the course of conversation Shiva itches to ask questions, but resists out of formality. Finally they head to the display. Somehow, encouraged by their quickening bonhomie, on the way Shiva plucks up the courage to ask, 'What do you do when you feel the temptations of the flesh? I hope you won't mind my asking; I felt I could ask you this as we have been discussing things on a purely intellectual plane.'

'It's all right, you need not explain, I understand that this question is bound to crop up in anyone's mind.' Mary looks unperturbed.

'Thanks. And so...?'

'I don't have to struggle to rationalise that sex is sin. This rationalisation helps me fight the temptation,' Mary says calmly.

'But still, sexual energy must be knocking hard at times.'

'The sexual energy is channelised into more sublimated ways; my sister and I fulfil each other's needs of affection and care, and yes, charity brings a lot of comfort, ' Mary says with conviction.

Shiva wonders if she is speaking her heart. '*She sounds pretty indoctrinated, speaking the language of a preacher*.' He suppresses the questions he still wants to ask.

They reach the display. Most of the members are also back. They find the guide explaining *The Last Judgment*. Shiva suddenly decides to listen to what the guide has to say about the other works of which he is not much aware. He tells Mary that he would share his views on *The Original Sin* later. With Mary's abstinence on his mind, he knows it would be a long deliberation. Mary nods, though a bit surprised. He takes the pictures of the replica with his mobile, so he can see them at leisure later. Mary notices frequent smiles on Shiva's face while the guide is briefing everyone. Now it's time for all to move into the galleries of the museum.

'Wow, it's just splendid, amazing... the walls, the pillars, the arches, the domes!' Shiva's remains agape at the fabled scultures—it exceeds everything he's read or been told about. Shiva is captivated by the classical grandeur of the white sculptures around, and human figures and colours on the ceiling. '*It is truly magic in motion! Stone heaving with soul.*' he exclaims to himself. Further on, in the corridors, the guide explains the histories of the famous artists and sculptors and their ouvre along the walls, the paintings and tapestries of great masters such as Botticelli, Ghirlandaio and Raphael. Shiva keenly watches the tapestries showing the 'baptism of Jesus', 'crucifixion of Jesus', and then on the 'coronation of Virgin Mary'. Here he stops for a while, removes his earplugs, and smilingly says to Mary while gazing at the tapestry, 'Marvellous!' Mary feels tempted to hear him more on this, but feels pressed to catch up with the guide with the help of the identity-flag in his hand; it's a huge mass of tourists inside. And finally they enter the famous Sistine Chapel to watch its ceiling depicting the Book of Genesis of Biblical fame. The origin of man remains an eternal question and a perpetual fascination too, to all humankind. A wry thought comes to him unbidden, '*The voluptuous women in the paintings and the sculptures—why don't they evoke lust, but the poetic perfection of the human body?*'

Shiva whispers to Mary his reflections on *The Original Sin* with a beginner's joke, 'Your original sin, not mine!' Suddenly, the mike blares at the amplifying whispers across the room, 'Please keep silent!' It's truly difficult for people to not speak out their feelings of wonder on seeing the ceiling. Shiva feels withdrawn, meditating upon the various ideas depicted there. The group remains for quite a while in the chapel before hearing the feeble voice of the guide on the audio, prompting the group members to come out as they are yet to cover their last destination, 'St Peter's Basilica'.

'Hah, so now I am eager to hear your impressions of *The Original Sin* at length,' Mary says settling into the chair in the roadside café they have chosen for their lunch after finishing their guided tour. Their friendship now trips along with informality—a common interest forges the surest and strongest bond between two individuals. Mary's commitment to sexual abstinence again surfaces in Shiva's mind.

Shiva has ordered for a beer and a pizza, while Mary has ordered bruchetta and lasagne along with a beer. Her ordering a beer excites Shiva, bringing alive the dinner with Zeba in Baku, when she refused alcohol of any kind.

'First let me hear your impressions, if you don't mind,' Shiva begins gently.

'Sure. It shows Eve tempted by the serpent into eating the forbidden fruit from the Tree of Knowledge despite God telling her not to. So, God turned angry at the disobedience of Eve—and Adam who too ate it later at her provocation—and cursed them with pain, expelling the two from the Garden of Eden; you have seen in the fresco how God drives them out,' Mary reminds Shiva.

'I never knew serpents could lure,' Shiva smiles teasingly.

'What do you mean?' Mary looks taken aback.

'Forget it. Do you agree that God is all-benevolent?'

'Of course, that goes without saying!'

'Then why would He ensnare man by creating the serpent and planting the Tree of Knowledge in the Garden of Eden, and yet ask him not to eat its tempting fruit?'

'But it was the serpent that convinced Eve, telling her that God forbade the eating of this fruit only because He didn't wish man should ever be able to tell right from wrong,' Mary argues.

'But the All-Benevolent creating such a vicious design doesn't sit well in my mind. Why would He allow the evil serpent to destroy, with his superior wiles, the innocence of Adam and Eve who He Himself created?'

'But it is written so.'

'I am not questioning that, just stating my views,' Shiva says, turning conscious of Mary's firm beliefs.

'Fine; you said God cursed man with pain as punishment for his sin. But would you know pleasure without pain? If we are eternally happy, won't it be like the sun never setting? And how would you explain the work we saw just a while ago, which showed God creating the sun and the moon, separating light from darkness?'

Mary remains silenced for a while before saying, 'Yes, a point to ponder.'

'And what pain do you think God gave him?' persisted Shiva.

'Man would not have known death but for his sin of disobedience.'

'But according to the Bible, did God not ask Adam and Eve to multiply?'

'Yes, he did.'

'Then just imagine how it would have been to keep multiplying without dying? Would this earth have not collapsed?' Shiva pauses for a while before a sarcastic smile flits across his face and he says, 'Or else did God plan to keep creating different earths at certain intervals?'

'So you find me funny.' Mary recognises the humour in the dichotomy.

'Oh, not at all.'

'But the death here is not physical, but spiritual, that's why Jesus had to atone for the sins of Man to revive the human spirit.' Mary sounds convinced by the weight of her own beliefs.

'Undeniably, Jesus atoned for the sin of man, but this sin was violence and unhappiness in the West Asian region where he was born; it was devastated by war and destruction. Before Jesus, didn't the teachings of Moses say almost the same thing? The New Testament of Christianity draws heavily from the Old Testament of Judaism. Did Buddha not preach non-violence and human good much before Jesus Christ?'

'But Jesus was not merely a man; he was the son of God, the divine messenger.'

'I feel he, like many of the others, was divine not in body but in his message, his deeds, in his service to humanity.'

'But then why are they described as divine?' Mary doesn't seem to relent.

'I think it's because seeking divine sanction helped their cause, as man is taught to obey the Divine without question.'

'But all who serve humanity aren't treated as divine.'

'An intelligent rebuttal, Mary. We try to, but since we know so much about the great people these days that it is difficult to treat them as God. I missed mentioning Mahatma Gandhi as the one who atoned for the sin of man with his death. I'm sure you have heard of him?'

'Of course I have; he got your country freedom with his non-violent Satyagraha,' Mary shows Shiva he is underestimating her knowledge.

'Wonderful. I'm sorry I misjudged you.'

'It's all right. Please continue.'

'Gandhi was not called God because we know so much about his birth and life. I believe history has engulfed God. Have you ever thought why God doesn't take incarnation anymore? That's why probably all those 'gods' resided in pre-history, where complete knowledge of a human being was not in the public domain, leaving a wide scope for speculation.'

Mary is listening to Shiva with rapt attention, admiration for his logic fighting with her faith.

Appreciating that it is very difficult to bring reason in the matter of God and religion, Shiva says again, 'Are you comfortable? Opinions do not have any religion; they are secular. Ours is merely an intellectual discussion.'

Finding Shiva appreciative of her sentiments and also finding some reason in what he says, Mary softens her stand. 'Yes, I am quite comfortable, please go on.'

'Coming back to the curse of pain, I read somewhere that had man not eaten the Forbidden Fruit, there would be no pain in childbirth. How would that be possible?'

'Frankly speaking, I am not aware of this interpretation.'

'Now I am curious to know what you think the sin of eating fruit actually caused?' Shiva can't help flushing.

'There are many views on this. It is said to have made man inherently disobedient to God without any sense of guilt. But I believe concupiscence is the fallout of the sin—after eating the fruit Adam and Eve first became conscious of their nakedness and then felt the rise of sexual attraction,' Mary says confidently.

'But how was it possible to multiply without the rise of sexual attraction in man? Or had God some other plan to bring about multiplication?'

Mary's expression assumes a neutral position.

There is a small pause before she says, 'It's amazing how you know so much about all of this!'

'Yes, it is my passion to know about different peoples, their mythologies, their traditions.'

'A corporate job and a love of mythology, a strange combination,' Mary muses with a puckish look.

'What I do for my livelihood is my ambition, and what I do for self-actualisation is my passion.'

They keep talking about their lives. Mary says, 'Do you know, I would love to visit India some time; your country fascinates me.'

'Anything particular that fascinates you?'

'I want to see the Taj Mahal, those grand forts and palaces of Rajasthan, and the exciting temples in the South, of course. One of my friends went to a place there to learn yoga and meditation. I find the history and tradition of your country very exciting and colourful,' Mary says warmly.

'Yes, it is. You are welcome to India. Please let me know when you come.'

'Yes, I would love to. But I want to say that you must visit my Florence too. That is the place the Renaissance began to flower, and great artists like Michelangelo and Leonardo Da Vinci came from. You would just love the Uffizi Gallery there, exhibiting the masterpieces of Renaissance art,' Mary says, reciprocating Shiva's offer of hospitality.

'As of now I am keen on a bit more of Rome,' Shiva gives a wide smile.

'How long is your stay?'

'I am leaving tomorrow; it's a late night flight. What about you?'

'I am leaving the day after.'

'What are your plans for tomorrow?' Shiva says.

'I shall see the Spanish Steps and the Trevi Fountain, and yes, do some shopping. Why don't you join me tomorrow if you can? I can show you these places.'

'It's like snatching a thought from my mind. Viewing Italy with an Italian—what could be better than that?' Shiva smiles a brilliant, grateful smile.

'You're welcome, Shiva,' she smiles back. Shiva likes hearing 'Shiva' in her accent. She checks her watch and says, 'I think I should leave now; I am spending this afternoon with my friends.'

'Sure. So tomorrow we meet at the Spanish Steps at 10?'

'That' s fine with me.'

They exchange their phone numbers to avoid any communication gap and part, with Mary thanking him for his exciting company.

Shiva gets back to his hotel room filled with thoughts of Mary. '*How inviting she looks! But she is not married, so she can't be my milestone... but is she not married?*' Shiva smiles to himself.

He rests for a while in his room before setting out again into the streets of Rome, taking in the multi-layered delights of the city. He finally sits in a café by the side of the River Tiber with some beer. He feels happy to be finally in the city he'd dreamt of visiting, a landmark which changed the way man thought and looked at himself, at God, and at the world. The beer turns his joy to meditation of history. '*The Renaissance taught man how to celebrate himself, it told man that he is at the centre of the universe, taught him to admire beauty for beauty's sake. Ah, the Mona Lisa! Telling man about the eternal beauty of life; that mysterious smile that man is still trying to decipher. Is she sad? Is she happy? Or else is it both at once? Did Mona Lisa not convey that life has to be enjoyed in both its shades, pain and pleasure, and thus treat it with equanimity? Who says beauty lies only in happiness? "Our sweetest songs are those that tell of saddest thought," wrote Shelley centuries later; the Renaissance taught man how to romance life, in pleasure as well as in pain.*'

He reaches the hotel with his blazing mind, Akriti, Sana, Zeba, all eclipsed.

'So how was meeting your friends?' Shiva asks the next day, his eyes taking in Mary clad in a white skirt and a sunshine-yellow short jacket over a sunshine-yellow tee, sporting a pony which lent a girlish look to her womanly figure. Her golden-yellow sunglasses, with bright maroonish lens add a generous dollop of glamour to her appearance.

'It was great.' Mary also can't help coolly admiring Shiva's well-maintained body, accentuated by his dark blue tight short tee. Shiva too is sporting glamorous shades.

They are sitting on the Spanish Steps amidst many people—more than usual as it's a Sunday.

'How was your day?'

'Good, but alone...' Shiva says giving her a mock-sad, puppy-dog look.

'Yes, I know, being alone in a strange place is bit of a drag.'

'Good we met again.'

'OK, let me tell you a bit about the Spanish Steps.' Shiva is the listener today. Mary is enjoying being at the other end.

She talks passionately about the area they are sitting in—'Did you know Keats's tomb is just a few feet from here?'—before she breaks off to suggest, 'Should we head to the Trevi Fountain?'

They walk on, having bought ice cream from a gelataria. On the way she makes him aware how famous a fountain Trevi is, not only in Rome but in the world, frequented by huge number of tourists. She explains, 'It's called Fontana Di Trevi in Italian; "trevi" means "three streets". It is supposed to mark the end of Rome's earliest aqueduct, Aqua Virgo, the source of pure water in ancient Rome. As per legend, a young virgin had showed this spring to some thirsty soldiers. Water from the fountain was carried to the Vatican too…' Mary feels passionate about letting Shiva know all about the fountain. They talk on while walking.

Shiva feels exhilarated by the sudden view of the grand sculptures—an assembly of statues of half-humans and rearing horses with the magnificent sea god Oceanus at their head, and aqua-green water at its base. It's thronged by art worshippers, and lovers who fling coins into the fountain to ensure they return to it one day. Shiva clicks a photo with his mobile. Mary feels happy at his happiness.

Mary continues speaking about the fountain, 'You can see the three statues which form the background; at the centre is Oceanus, the god of the sea, to its left is the goddess of abundance, and the one to its right is the goddess of health.' Shiva observes them keenly, listening to Mary. He can't help marvelling at the fine intricate detailing of the marble.

'Anything fascinating?' Mary asks him, finding him trying to see something minutely.

'I was just wondering, what is this snake doing here?' Shiva points to the statue of Sirona—the goddess of health—at the right of Oceanus, showing a snake drinking from a bowl.

'I can recall, on my first tour, that the guide had said that Romans believed snakes to be symbols of health and healing because of their ability to shed their skin,' Mary says, turning smug.

Shiva has a typical put-down ready. 'Yesterday the snake in the Vatican was evil and today it's good.'

'Always pondering you are,' Mary smiles unperturbed at him.

'By the way, what is this coin-dropping about?' Shiva asks, seeing a few people, with their back to the fountain, throwing coins over their shoulders.

'It's believed that throwing coins fulfil your wishes, but the wishes are fixed.' Mary says excitedly.

'Fixed?'

'Yes; throwing one coin over the right shoulder ensures your return to Rome, two, means a love affair with an attractive Italian, and three, marriage with an Italian.'

Suddenly Mary finds Shiva making his way through the people. He goes down near the railing lining the pool, turns his back to the fountain, and throws two coins into it in quick succession.

'Do you recall what throwing two coins ensures?' Mary asks him from some distance.

'Yes, very much,' Shiva says, his eyes sparkling with a shy hue of coquetry.

Mary looks at him, feeling amused and uneasy at once. She doesn't make any further query, which disappoints Shiva. Mary has drawn herself near him.

'What next? I'm hungry,' Shiva says to lighten the atmosphere.

'Trevi street has very good restaurants; I know one that serves delicious home-made pasta which pairs so well with Italian wine.'

'Let's go!' exults Shiva.

They go. Mary tells him more on the way about other attractions of Rome. Shiva expresses his desire to visit Italy again, clubbing it with the other destinations of Italy like Florence and Venice. Talking on, they settle into the restaurant of Mary's recommendation. They thoroughly enjoy their lunch. Shiva relishes their turning freer with each other, the kick from the wine helping things along pretty well. Lunch over, now was the time for dispersal. But Mary tells him to stay a bit longer because they still have some time left before her friend joins her at a place which is not far from Trevi; her friend is taking off from work in the afternoon to join her for some shopping.

Somehow, throughout their togetherness today, Shiva has thought of Mary as actually being another milestone on his journey, a journey towards the discovery of marriage not between two individuals, but that between an individual and her belief. Shiva is disappointed, and steels himself to work harder on Mary. He knows cerebral qualities instantly attract women, and Mary seems already attracted. He reflects, '*The cocktail of logic and looks is lethal. It can kill a woman with sheer desire. Mary may also…*' He allows himself a self-conceited smile.

He turns to Mary to say, 'Seeing *The Original Sin* with you yesterday was a great pleasure. You know, the pleasure derived from a duel between two contrasting opinions is matchless. I would not have enjoyed expressing this perspective to someone who already believed in what I said; life can't be enjoyed without contrasts.'

'How did you learn to speak so well? And more than that, how do you sound so convinced and peaceful, while professing the thoughts which are contrary to general belief?' Mary sounds awed, thrilling Shiva.

'*She doesn't know about the black hole in my mind or how troubling it is! But she is growing impressed. Can I attain this woman from the country of the Renaissance?*'

'Nothing so special about it,' he says aloud. I like to debate, to argue—even with myself. If you don't mind I want to tell you something more on *The Original Sin.*' He sips his coffee, the strategy propelling him on.

'Yes, please.'

'You know, we treat God as one, irrespective of the many religions man has created. Do you agree?'

'Yes.'

'In our mythology we have Lord Brahma who is supposed to have created the universe, this Earth and life on it. After creating Earth, He, by His wisdom, gave birth to Kama Deva from His own mind. Therefore, He is also the lord of kama which means desire, what you call concupiscence, without which man could not have conceived future generations, and Earth could not be sustained. So how can one god treat desire as sin and another as need? Is my question a reasonable one?

'Yes; but then how can you believe Brahma to be God?' Mary asks frankly.

'Exactly, this is the point I want to make: it's all mythology. Brahma's story is like the story of Adam and Eve. People created it with their imagination, and different people thought differently in their own ways; it is again the freedom to name the nothingness. I feel tempted to find some logic in all this, which I feel would definitely appeal to you.'

'What is that?' Mary asks.

'Can nothingness, this void what we call God, be divided in terms of geography? I mean, can space have a boundary? Evidently, no. Your religion says God is one; in that case how is the Christian God different from the Hindu or the Islamic God?'

'True,' says Mary briefly, wanting him to continue.

'Now, do you feel like having a relook at your interpretation of the 'original sin'? Logically it can't be sex.'

'I am still convinced about it.' Belief reclaims Mary.

Arresting his thoughts in order not to offend Mary,

Shiva says, 'All said and done, my intention was not to influence your belief. It's just that I was enjoying the debate. I will sum it up by saying that whatever grows naturally in man, like desire does, cannot be sinful, and ultimately God is also nature. And yes, to understand what I say better, please do visit Khajuraho when you visit India.' And then he tells her a bit about Khajuraho. Finally, both smile at each other, in readiness to part.

Shiva shakes his head and tells himself, '*She is too strongly entrenched in her belief to fall for my logic.*' He feels sad, defeated too, thinking, '*Did she not feel any physical attaction for me*? *Could she not read in my hard persuasion my interst in her*?' He notices a certain sadness in Mary's eyes. They exchange their email addresses and promise to remain in touch.

He goes back to the hotel to freshen up. He chats with Sana; he had received quite a few messages from her. He phones his home just a little later, ascertaining everyone's well-being. Off and on, he has felt homesick, missing Ankur, and Akriti too, figuring in a hazy blur.

The rest of the day for Shiva is about getting the general feel of Rome, buying gifts at the airport for Ankur and Akriti, souvenirs for his friends, saying goodbye to Rome, and finally drinking in a heady cocktail of solitude and beer.

But at the end, the sense of 'losing' Mary adds a darker shade to his black hole.

# Mary Flowers into a Lotus

Shiva's perception of his own journey remains a strange mix of the sacred and the sinister: sinister denoting his means of seducing women away from wedlock, and sacred, his goal of achieving a complete understanding of the institution of marriage—whether of bodies or of minds.

But like any journey of discovery, Shiva's also is as much a matter of deed as of destiny. Sana is the success of deed with the support of destiny, while Zeba, a flash of destiny, and Mary, apparently the failure of his determined deed which remained unsupported by destiny. While he comes off the plane after landing at Delhi, Sana comes to the fore of his mind, soothing the heartache caused by his failure in Italy.

Shiva returns to his routine in Delhi: home, gym, office and Sana. But the Sana he returns to is not the same; guilt from his trysts with Zeba and Mary keeps needling him. His mind is a maelstrom of emotions, it remains a black hole.

'Since your return, I find you a bit absentminded,' Sana says. She is making her ritual visit to his chamber in the morning.

'Is that so?'

'Yes, anything wrong?'

'I can't think of anything.' Shiva knows that he is lying; the loss of Mary heads his list of griefs at this juncture of his life.

'You know, when you were away, I could sense even the inanimate things we shared come alive with your imagined presence: the sofa, the bed, the rooms.'

'I missed you terribly, too,' says Shiva.

They converse on.

Almost six months have elapsed since he returned from Italy. During this time, he has taken his family on a pleasant vacation to Himachal, and has met Sana thrice at her home. But he always sensed a blurred image of his Venus by his side.

'Dear Shiva,

Do you remember me? Hope this finds you fine and doing well in both your work and on your passionate voyage through the oceans of the gods. I want to inform you that I have planned my visit to India during the latter half of the coming December, and believe me, you were the first one who sprang to mind when I thought of India. I still cherish seeing the Sistine Chapel with you and new eyes. May I request you to please guide me on how best to plan my itinerary in your country? As I told you, I am keen on seeing the Taj Mahal, the forts and palaces of Rajasthan, and of course the Khajuraho you recommended my going to. Would love to see India through your eyes, or with new eyes, again.

With warm regards,
Mary,
Florence, Italy'

Shiva remains buried in his laptop all night. He thinks, '*How to tell you, Mary, I remember* everything *about you. Your face is engraven in my mind. The defeat I experienced when my logic did not touch upon your belief still has me in its grip. I believe that when a woman loses such a battle, she loses her heart, and maybe, her body also.*'

'Dear Mary,

I am just delighted to hear from you. It is really heartening to know you have finally decided to visit India. Let me assure you, you will fall in love with the diversity in this country's people and places. I will be only too happy to guide you through your stay and, if possible, may accompany you also to a place or two. In view of my project hotting up, time may be an issue. But rest assured

I will be waiting eagerly for you to come. Please send me your dates when they are finalised. Welcome to India,

Warm regards,

Shiva

Delhi, India'

Time has again swept Shiva deep under the spell of Mary. The march up to December feels tedious; he is counting the days. The human heart clings to the faintest hope.

'So, finally India has brought you here!' Shiva says joyfully to Mary. They are sitting in the lobby of the hotel where Mary is putting up at Delhi, smiling like lovers at each other.

'Yes, of course! Didn't you believe me when I told you that I was planning a visit to India?' Mary enjoys the expression on Shiva's face.

'Well… Anyway, nice to see you again.' They are still holding each other's hands; the longer the distance covered for a meeting, the greater the thrill.

'So, how are you placed for time?'

'Have you planned your journey? Your mail didn't tell me much.'

'Not entirely, I wanted to leave some flexibility for you. To begin with, I have finalised the details of my trip to Rajasthan.'

'That's fine. You can manage Rajasthan on your own. There are good professional guides to take you through all the forts and palaces you want. In Khajuraho and, maybe, Agra, too, I will try to join you.' Shiva's mind has already started cooking up an alibi for remaining away from home; it will be 'an official trip'.

'Because you wish to show me the fusion of godliness and desire,' Mary quotes deliberately from their old conversation.

'Believe me, Khajuraho is unique in many respects,' Shiva says seriously.

'Would you like to have dinner with me?' Mary asks.

'No, thanks, I came to you straight from my office. I could manage coming here as you are staying near the airport which is not very far from my place; the folks at home would be waiting for dinner.'

'It's all right.'

'So here it is: you leave for Rajasthan tomorrow as you have planned, and come back to Delhi when you like. But, please inform me a bit in advance; you can call me too. From here I will accompany you to Khajuraho. On the way back, we can visit Agra and the Taj. Delhi, you can keep for the last.'

They finalise the dates before Shiva takes leave of Mary.

So, finally the day has come when Shiva and Mary are flying to Khajuraho. Shiva has booked a room for himself in the hotel where Mary has planned to stay.

They rush through the sandy expanse to the complex of temples. Mary stares around in disbelief. 'Oh, my God! It's so explicit! And that too on the sacred walls of temples?' Mary gapes at the erotic sculptures.

'Did I fail to convey this to you in Rome?' Shiva relishes her awe.

'Not that; even I saw a few pictures on the internet, but seeing it for real is a different experience altogether.'

'What are your impressions?'

'These carvings are marvellous. How did they portray such complex figures and postures in stone? They look like they're breathing! I am loving it!' Mary gasps out the words, rather naughty for her.

'I told you it's unique in many respects; art holds many wonders.'

But a slight shyness from seeing those sexually explicit scenes with Shiva is pretty noticeable on her face; she shifts her glance from Shiva to the walls, and hastily back.

'So this is the fusion you talked of in Rome.'

'Precisely, yes. I want to stress the fact that desire is sacred, and secular too; a biological reality can't be a sin. You can see up there that, along with sex, other routine activities of life have also been depicted, women doing themselves up, putting on ornaments and so on, which suggest that sex is just one of the normal activities of human life. Khajuraho dissolves the dichotomy between erotica and eternity,' Shiva concludes with conviction.

'That is something debatable. I came across another perspective while reading about these sculptures before coming here,' Mary says, grinning impishly.

'I am curious to know.'

'The erotica has been displayed only on the outer walls of these temples; it suggests that the sinful thoughts of sex had to be shed from the mind before entering the sanctum for the worship of God.'

'I'm afraid I don't agree, and again I have sound logic on my side. Do you find any sense of struggle emerging from the expressions of the men and women portrayed here? Just look up there and notice the bliss on their faces; how well it resonates with the sense of prosperity conveyed by the women wearing ornaments and preening themselves!' Such experimental postures can be the handiwork of happiness only.' Shiva draws Mary's attention to some specific sculptures of the Lakshmana temple.

Mary's thoughts are provoked by Shiva's arguments. She turns an admiring gaze into his eyes.

'But please tell me why I shouldn't take it as a whim of the Chandela rulers of that time.' Mary sounds well-conversant with Indian history. She has done some thorough homework, as Westerners do before visiting a place.

'Yes, of course you are free to think that way. But don't my arguments appeal to your reason? Interpretation must stand the test of logic. I can cite another interpretation which appeals to *my* reason.'

'Do explain.'

'How blissful communion with the divine feels, has to remain a matter of man's conjecture. I read somewhere, when I had come here last, that the blissful sexual union depicted here suggests that sex is the only human experience which can stand a comparison with the bliss imagined to be provided by a spiritual union with God.'

'That's pretty speculative.'

'Speculation is the divine itself. Didn't we agree at the Sistine that God is about naming the nothingness?'

'Yes, we did, but…'

'I haven't finished. These erotic sculptures may also convey that unless you have experienced sexual pleasure frequently and intensely enough to get bored with it, you can't aim at the pure divine,' says Shiva, watching keenly for her reaction.

'But all these, you say, are things you read somewhere; where is the Shiva Special?' Mary also turns puckish, and a little greedy, thinking her 'Lonely Planet' would have never given such exciting views on Khajuraho. '*If only I could travel with him everywhere!*' She didn't enter a convent because she could live her freedom, and travel the world; she was fine with the vow of chastity, but not the vow of disobedience.

'For that, let me take you to another temple which is called the Devi Jagdamba temple.' Shiva is relieved that Mary has lightened up.

When they arrive there, Shiva announces with a flourish, 'This is my favourite temple in Khajuraho. More than the erotic sculptures, something else fascinates me here.'

'Should I make a request to hear that?' Mary's curiosity rises to the bait, but with humour.

'As you move in,' Shiva explains as they go along, 'you come across the statues of Brahma, Vishnu and Shiva in the order I named them. They form the trinity of Hindu mythology…' Mary nods here, suggesting she knows that. Shiva says again, 'I told you in Rome about Brahma, the creator of the Universe, and how he produced from his mind Kama Deva, the god of desire, so that man could multiply, and human life on Earth could continue. Likewise, Vishnu is believed to be the preserver and Shiva the destroyer of the universe.'

'Yes, I can recall some of that.'

'Perfect, now if your patience permits, I want to tell you a short story.'

'I would love to hear it,' Mary prods him.

'Lord Shiva lost his wife, Sati. Out of grief, He sat in meditation. Around the same time, Indra and the other gods were feeling threatened by the demon Tarkasur who was out to decimate the gods—hope you know devas and asuras constantly fight in Hindu mythology—and it was held by the gods that only the offspring of Shiva could defeat Tarkasur. Shiva had no son from his first wife, Sati. Hence Kama Deva—the lord of desire—was sent by Brahma to induce desire in Shiva by shooting his arrow of flowers into him. Shiva opened his eyes and beheld the beautiful Parvati, whom the gods had sent to induce Shiva out of his trance, waiting on Him. Ultimately, Shiva married her, and the fruit of their union, Karthikeya, killed Tarkasur.

But, angry with Kama for spoiling his meditation, Shiva burnt him with his eyes. Then Lord Vishnu, the preserver of the order of life, pleaded with Parvati to ask Shiva to bring Kama Deva back to life, as he knew that life cannot exist without desire. Though Shiva resurrected Kama Deva, he did not bless him with a body, and instead allowed him to exist only in spirit. In the end, Vishnu caused Kama Deva's spirit to enter into his human incarnate form, as Krishna's son, Pradyumna.

Can you guess the wisdom in this knowledge? And that wisdom is what will be the Shiva Special.' The human Shiva's eyes sparkle.

'Will you tell me?' Mary asks a little weakly.

'Brahma, the creator of the universe, created desire. Vishnu, the preserver, preserved desire by lending

Krishna's body and seed to Kama Deva. And Shiva, the destroyer, destroyed desire by burning Kama Deva. Thus is established the truth of sex being the source of creation. The day it ceases to exist, the universe will collapse.'

Mary looks enchanted by the story. For a very brief moment, her belief, that sex is sinful, is shaken. But no later, her faith makes a comeback. What stays with her is the exhilarating beauty of her own Shiva's mind. '*Can't beauty be an end in itself?*' her mind repeats the rhetoric to herself over the day.

'You know what has impressed me the most so far?' Mary asks Shiva. 'It is that there is no end to deriving perspectives from a piece of art; nobody can know absolutely what the artist wanted to convey through his creation.'

Shiva agrees with her but is disturbed by the thought that his mission to transform Mary's belief is yet not accomplished; somewhere inside him he feels that winning Mary's belief would mean winning not only her mind, but heart and body too.

'But I feel a bit confused here,' Mary continues from before. 'It also means that no belief system can be absolute either.'

Shiva is overjoyed. 'Mary, you are unconsciously guiding the discussion to the truth I want to bring out,' he says with a victorious smile.

'I didn't get you.' They've been walking on the platform of the temple, around the sanctum, for quite a while.

'What I'm trying to say is that if one belief could cater to all human minds, what was the need for so many belief systems, and so many philosophical schools? Each school of philosophy is pivoted on some particular belief. While one says God exists, the other says there is nothing called God; while one says that this human world is illusory, the other says it is the only reality; while one condemns sensual pleasure, the other upholds it.' Shiva deliberately concludes his diatribe with 'sensual pleasure' because that is what he wants to bring Mary to.

Suddenly a sense of déjà vu returns: the thought of Einstein's endeavour to explain all the phenomena of the universe in terms of a single equation, the thought of the politico-economic orders—the various permutations and combinations of capitalism and communism—devised so far being imperfect, which hit him during the Baku visit, and the thought of the marital orders like monogamy and polygamy being insufficient, which emerged after his trysts with Sana and Zeba.

'Yeah, that is all very well, but now let's go in and see your gods.' Mary is already moving inside the sanctum, but can't help and asks quizzically, 'Do you believe in so many gods?' Being a Christian Mary knows God to be One.

'We already talked on this; you can lend any form to nothingness with your imagination, and believing in many gods has a huge advantage,' Shiva smiles enigmatically.

'What's that?'

'The variety in gods affords man the facility to assign them various human characteristics, so that he can remain at peace with himself, believing "Whatever I do, some god did before me, and so, it is natural".' Shiva throws his head back laughing at a personal memory: once, in a debating competition during his college days, he had argued against polytheism in the Hindu religion—and won the first prize—and here he was, arguing in its favour!

Mary rejoices in his laughter, but not without shyly noticing the sudden attention of the people around in the temple.

They wander at length through the several temples of Khajuraho before Mary feels exhausted by the exertion and the heat and wants to go back to the hotel for some rest. They have got a day more at their disposal in Khajuraho. They decide to have lunch at their hotel. Shiva orders a beer while Mary a soft drink before lunch; an afternoon beer dispels the tiredness of the day for Shiva. They keep talking, rejoicing over their findings in Khajuraho, over lunch.

Finally, they go to their respective rooms, having decided to move out in the cool of the evening for another leisurely excursion.

Mary lies in her bed, and gradually sinks into slumber. The thoughts expressed by her friend during their visit to the temples are floating in her mind, the extreme respect she feels for him keeps her smiling. She senses a strange enchantment possessing her, which she finds thrilling and disturbing at once; '*Is it his logic impregnating my belief?*' No, it is just her adoration of his beautiful mind. She is suddenly startled and sits up alert on the bed with a sense of the bizarre.

Shiva is in his room. '*I could sense her admiration for me in her eyes,*' he thinks gleefully, '*but I have not given her any strong hint of my real intentions. And I don't think I could break her belief in chastity. Not every time can logic emerge a victor. Her apparent attraction is not physical...*' The recurring feeling of defeat keeps him restless for the rest of the afternoon. But still, the thought that Mary has completely conquered her desire for sex and is at absolute peace with herself continues to challenge his understanding of human nature.

They set out in the evening. Shiva finds Mary's calculated reserve suddenly mellowed into a totally informal demeanor. In between jesting and generally making merry, she jocularly pats his back; while crossing roads she unconsciously holds his hand... '*It is the last opportunity to win Mary*', Shiva warns himself. He lavishly returns her friendly touches and pats and by dinner time they appear like old schoolpals.

'I want to share something if it is OK with you,' Shiva smiles at her across their table in a restaurant they have gone to for their dinner.

'Sure, please...' Mary also smiles.

'I wanted to say this in Rome itself, but then I felt we had not been friends long enough.'

'Come on, don't hesitate. Aren't we bosom pals now?'

'I feel you are a woman who has directly stepped out of a Renaissance painting.' Shiva's gaze sweeps her figure. She looks wonderful in the all-black sari she has dressed up in, with dangling earrings, a pendant necklace around her neck, a bindi adorning her forehead, and her golden hair left untied to fall to her shoulders. Shiva feels charmed by the sight of a Western woman decked up in ethnic Indian wear.

'Oh really?' Mary tries to hide her blush. 'You're embarrassing me.'

'Many Italians would be disappointed in finding the "no entry" barricade you have displayed before you,' Shiva lends humour to his flirting; humour makes flirtation legitimate and safe.

She giggles, blushing deeply all the while, but doesn't utter a word. Shiva, taking her laughter as reciprocation, says again, 'Desire would feel deprived in not finding expression through such a beautiful woman.' He then eyes her over his glass of wine, testing her response.

'Desire feeling deprived...?'

'Yes, Ms Mary.'

'Is there anything on earth that you cannot philosophise over?' she says a little sharply. 'Although you *do* have a way with words, I admit.'

'I sincerely meant all I said but if you don't like it, I will reserve my opinions,' Shiva says sportingly.

'Not at all, Shiva; in fact, I am enjoying it all thoroughly.'

'Shall I say something more then?'

'Sure.'

'Don't you ever feel the need to express your desires?'

All her life, Mary has satisfied her puritan self by killing all thoughts of sex before they even started. Tonight also, she changes the subject. After chatting a little longer, she suggests a stroll since they have finished eating.

'Sure,' Shiva says dispiritedly.

They walk aimlessly around till they find themselves in a deserted area of the city behind the temple; it is a nondescript playground of a small town. They come across an open and wide expanse and sit on a cemented circular plinth which is cast around the centre of a sandalwood tree. Shiva briefly ponders the belief that '*sandalwood trees attract snakes*'. A ripe moon scatters silver into the darkness. They resume their discussion of the erotic sculptures they have seen.

She stands up abruptly, faces Shiva, and guides one of his hands to her breasts, Shiva's apples. He can feel her heart throbbing under them. '*Breasts are the true speakers of a woman's heart*' crosses his mind again. He feels lust coursing through his veins at the speed of a cobra's venom. Simultaneously, she plants a kiss on his lips. It is like teasing a hornets' nest. Shiva grabs Mary's buttocks in a flash, his hands moving quickly upward back to her breasts, traversing her body with unexpected freedom. He kisses her lips, face, neck; in no time, his hands are crazily trying to release her apples—which had been forbidden for so long.

'Yes, come on, discover in me Renaissance art and Khujuraho sculptures all at once,' Mary gasps, thrusting herself forward, lending all of her body for his discovery.

'Oh Mary, you don't know how desperately I have been craving you,' Shiva's words struggle for utterance.

'I know, otherwise how could I offer myself without being sure of your attraction for me? Come on, define desire for me.' The whiff of her newly-stirred desires maddens him. '*Such a potent scent can be raised only by a maiden melt,*' Shiva can't help reflecting even amidst his frenzy.

Their bodies are bathed by the moonlight into living sculptures themselves.

Finally, Shiva comes to take full possession of Mary, her appetite transformed from sin to sanctity. The whiff of her desire permeates the air around them, with Shiva reflecting, '*How intoxicating it feels to know my logic has melted her belief!'* The thought adds fuel to his fire, until he collapses inside her, shouting in his ecstasy, all thoughts of Akriti forgotten.

They rearrange their clothes, and walk back to the hotel, still with their arms around each other, no intrusive eyes to disturb their peace. In the hotel, they enter Shiva's room without exchanging a word, their bodies struggling to dominate each other. They make love all night, Shiva rejoicing in the thrill of the rollercoaster ride over the steep slopes between her depths and her rises. For Mary, being with Shiva since the last evening has not only meant being baptised into desire, but graduating in it straight away; the endeavor to unwrap the gifts of nature is sublimely effortless.

Waking up in the morning, they remain in bed, still sensing much to be discovered in each other. The curtains in the room remain drawn, sustaining the translucent hue of their passionate night into the day.

They leave the room only for a lunch they suddenly feel ravenous for, returning almost at once to resume their games of love in a painted afternoon. The pattern of movement is repeated till they realise that two whole days have passed in a flash. '*Time dilation*' springs to Shiva's mind again.

They separate at Khajuraho airport when Shiva has to fly back to Delhi, called by his office, while Mary travels to Agra for her visit to the Taj. They will meet again before her final departure. Their reunion in Delhi is now a foregone conclusion.

'So the time has come to leave,' Mary says to Shiva sadly. They are at the Delhi airport as Mary has to catch her flight to Rome.

'Not to worry, we will remain in touch,' Shiva chokingly reciprocates her feelings.

'But, you know, a sense of guilt pricks me now; I wish it were not there!'

'I still remember you saying at the Lotus Temple that your favourite flower is a lotus. Tell me how can you get to a lotus bloom without wading through some muddy water? The path to the lotus of such sublime desire has to pass through the muddy waters of guilt.'

'You and your way with words,' Mary smiles with glistening eyes.

'May I ask you something?'

'Do you require permission even now?' Mary asks with love in her eyes.

'Could you be convinced that sex is not a sin?'

'I just answered this question.'

Shiva looks amazed at her. After a smiling pause, she says, 'I feel if my belief were transformed, guilt wouldn't rise in me; sex with you was a tribute to the beauty of your mind.'

Her words cause an instant blow to his sense of winning Mary.

Hearing the announcement for her flight, Mary begins walking away without another word into the departure area. Shiva stands still, waiting a long time for a last glimpse of her.

Returning from the airport, sitting in his car, thinking of the desire drying up between him and Akriti, Sana's surfing waters kissing the shores of desire, Zeba's thorny access to the rose of desire, Mary's maiden tryst with the lotus of desire through guilt-ridden muddy waters, all lie in an inextricable mix in Shiva's mind; the black hole stays put.

☒

# Black Hole Turns Radiant

Is truth an intellectual discovery? Or is it a divine revelation? Can truth also be invented? Is Shiva not trying to invent truth with his mind, logic and experience?

Shiva moans at night in his bed, it is the day Mary left. He is reminded of Deven again. During his last two visits they have not been able to meet for long and he has eagerly awaited his next trip. Over the weeks, Deven has been updated only upto Shiva's encounter with Mary in Rome.

Life in Delhi has resumed; his unspoken accord with Akriti has now stabilised; both have rationalised 'living apart together', the occasional spikes in Shiva's anger against her notwithstanding. His relationship with Sana has assumed a level, having fallen into a routine of occasional meetings, which remain far and few, leaving him guilt-ridden.

'So ultimately you emerge a victor…' Deven says to Shiva. They are sitting in a restaurant in Gurgaon. Shiva has told him about his conquest of Mary.

'But I feel restless,' Shiva says, and then explains to Deven about the persistent black hole in his mind. He sips his scotch with a grave contortion of his lips, as if styling his scotch to his somber moods.

'Even after your screw going global?' Deven shakes with chuckles.

'Buddy, you find it funny,' Shiva's depression deepens.

'But what makes you sad now? Your journey testifies that traditions do not sufficiently match with human chemistry, and that is what you wanted to establish.'

'It's a strange gloom.'

'I told you earlier that digging mythology, history and tradition with the spade of reason is bound to be hazardous,' Deven says, sobering down.

'You're probably right. Tradition tends to militate against reason, and sometimes, against happiness too.'

'So shed the sadness, and relish the experiences you voyaged so far for.'

'But how to get rid of this black hole? It torments me,' Shiva's angst grows louder. He says again, 'But while I too seek some shore, I am afraid of my journey ending. I long, too, to meet a man who is really happy.'

'If at all such a man exists,' Deven says pessimistically, but quickly adds, 'Bro, as for now I would advise you to end your journey because it can be physically hazardous. You only said that you indulged in unguarded passions also, though I understand the subjects of your study were all safe so far, but...' Deven takes a reflective pause before saying again 'Now document your journey. This I am telling you from my own experience of writing some poetry. Releasing your thoughts gives you great relief; it lends some coherence to your unruly mind. The rain of gloomy thoughts gives rise to the rainbow of happiness,' Deven speaks from his heart, under the spell of a poetic efflorescence, taking a big draught of scotch.

'That crossed my mind too.'

'So get going and document your screwing journey.' Deven is again convulsed with laughter.

Shiva returns the humour through a gentle smile. Suddenly he feels the thought of having relished the varied flavours of passion filling him with smugness.

'I will write for sure; how can I challenge the verdict of a writer on how writing feels,' Shiva says in a cheerier mood.

Shiva shifts the focus to Deven's new venture. He feels happy to learn that it takes off next month. They keep chatting over their dinner before dispersing. Deven has to fly back to Mumbai early in the morning.

Shiva returns home, his mind already trying to figure out a scheme for writing in the hectic schedule of his life and work. He resolves to get started from that very night. From here on, all his energies and time will be channelised into documenting his journey, which will not be without frustrating breaks in the flow. But the writing itself lends some warmth to his chilled heart.

Tonight, he struggles with the conclusion: '… why did I feel committed to Sana and guilty about getting physical with Zeba when me and Sana were not tied by any sacramental bond? Guilt there emerged from conscience rather than tradition; I could sense godliness in conscience. The three marriages I could study—mine, Sana's and Zeba's—revealed that conscience didn't approve adherence to the order. There was no reason for me, Sana and Zeba to feel guilty in stepping out of our respective marriages to fulfil our sexual urges—Akriti turned adulterous, the husbands of Sana and Zeba didn't command respect, and thus lost the fidelity of their wives. How happily those women turned to my embrace! Yes, sex of course remains a major issue in one's life, but with due respect to the spouse, it fades with time. But then again, it is the conscience which guides an individual on his path, since no traditional order can delineate a universal path. The interplay of sex, trust, respect, and love in a marriage may brew an emotion—it subsumes fidelity—which I feel varies from individual to individual; one has to deduce one's own truth.

'During my journey, I felt forced to question myself over a myriad things: right and wrong, pain and pleasure, desire and guilt, God and man, tradition and human chemistry, choose, choose, choose, all of which adds up to a black hole.

Now, most importantly coming to Akriti, who powered this voyage. However, I am not sure whether I wouldn't have turned adulterous but for her adultery. But what I am sure about is that in the absence of the desire for revenge, which has a definite streak of narcissism, this journey wouldn't have been what it turned out to be—a journey of discovering marriage and desire, and what lies between.

I call my approach to Akriti's adultery passively vengeful, because it didn't lead to any direct confrontation with her, nor did it lead to our separation, and remained subdued at the level of anger. Yes, the anger against her remains with me, and may sustain itself for ever. My intellectual endeavour to view my wife as a woman first, and a human being still before that kept getting challenged by the 'husband' in me, who wanted to command the eternal subservience of the body of his wife. I couldn't even bring myself to stop having those occasional bouts of bitterness against her. But yes, at this juncture, in retrospect, I can also safely say that this anger couldn't kill my soft sentiments for her, which I feel confused in naming. Is this anger the manifestation of my affinity with her? And can I also infer that besides Ankur, these sentiments have significantly contributed to the continuance of our togetherness? I kept guessing that the reason for her adultery might be boredom, but never tried to know the exact rationale. I feel it might have brought about the consequences which my reason has so far successfully precluded. And reviving passions with her also never seemed an effective idea, as sex anyway had escaped from our lives, regardless of whether Akriti had an affair or not.'

Shiva stops typing, asking himself in the midst of rambling, '*Why do you want to comprehend and judge your thoughts and actions in such a simplistic way? The coherence you seek will never come; the perspective Deven talked about is that absolute truth is not always extricable as it lies in inaccessible gaps and fissures of the mind, and this disorderliness of the mind is the actual order. Not every turmoil ends in quietitude. But you still couldn't resist the temptation of drawing a coherent conclusion from your journey—at your peril—and see how you have ended up projecting yourself as an intellectual Goliath!*'

Finally, he concludes inconclusively.

The journey of documentation has finally ended. It has taken quite a few months for him to complete it. But in spite of the rain of Shiva's gloomy thoughts, Deven's 'rainbow of happiness' doesn't rise in his mind; the black hole refuses to shift residence.

Shiva is suddenly struck with some urgent official matter. He opens his laptop to send a mail. As soon as he opens his mail box, he comes across a mail from Mary, saying, 'Dear Shiva, here is a surprise for you—finally I experience the birth…'

The black hole explodes into a radiant star.

☒